FATHERS COME FIRST

To my darling Chupi and Luke

Fathers Come First

ROSITA SWEETMAN

THE LILLIPUT PRESS
DUBLIN

Published in 2014 by
The Lilliput Press,
62–63 Sitric Road,
Dublin 7, Ireland
www.lilliputpress.ie

ISBN: 978 1 84351 6347

A clip record for this title is available from The British Library.

10 9 8 7 6 5 4 3 2 1

Typeset in 11.5 pt Bembo by Susan Waine
Printed in Navarre, Spain, by GraphyCems

PART ONE

There are important things to remember. All the time, though, the remembering and the importance changes. Depending. Depending where you are, who you're with. Why.

I used to think sleeping with men was very important. I used to say to myself: Well now, when I've done that, that will be really something.

I used to think growing up would be important. I'd think: When I'm twenty, life will seem very solid. Life will be like a library, or a church. Full of shades and subtleties and things stacked away, neat and jumbled, both.

I used to think church one of *the* most important things. God was enormous and took up most of the sky and shouted. God sat over the altar in church and watched you. Church made your face change, made it stiff and long. It made women whisper and your stepmother very tetchy if you asked to borrow her handkerchief.

I used to think my stepmother terribly important. I used to lie awake at night and swear by the Holy God and Sweet Jesus and Dear Our Lady, that I would leave home, run away, hide. I would hope and think of my stepmother wandering the whole earth looking for me, begging me to return. People would say, Well if you'd been nicer to her you know…

I used to think what people said was important. I used to ask friends, 'What does Valerie *really* think of me?' I used to cry and say, 'Nobody really likes me' and wait for all the girls to come and hug me and say, 'We do, we do.'

Later on I used to think what men said was important. I used to spend hours thinking about what they might or might not say.

I used to feel a fool, a failure, a factory reject if they didn't say, 'You're the greatest, the most beautiful, the sexiest girl we've ever met.'

I used to think being a wife, a Mrs, vastly important. Perhaps so important that you didn't think about it too much—all effort was bent towards it, like rivers and streams move towards the sea, quickly or slowly, naturally.

I never thought jobs were that important. Jobs were for important people—like men, so's they could bring home fur coats and delicatessen food to their wives and talk about difficult things at dinner parties. I thought, Jobs, oh well, jobs.

I never thought money important. Money was a huge safe that men had the key to and you just had to get a man and then you got the money. Some men got a lot, some a little; you just had to choose the right man. First there were fathers, and then there were boyfriends, and then there were lovers, and then you thought, Well then there'll be husbands. Certainly money wasn't important.

You start off I suppose thinking you yourself the most important thing in the whole world. You get given a big breast and you suck it right into your face and hold it with your baby hands and you're satisfied.

Then your parents become important. They watch you, and you them. They give a little and then stop and then give a little more. It's not like the breast. You don't feel that full, that satisfied, ever again.

You get cranky and you always stay that way because once you knew what *enough* really was, so you carry that idea round in your head, but you never get it again. Really you never learn how to get it again.

But. You've got your mother and your father. They're very careful of you. They know about your disappointment and they try to help you. They've been through it. You don't realize that till much later—you think they're just dog-in-the-mangers. Meaners.

My mother died when I was four. I think that must have been quite important. I didn't have the breast then and I didn't have her. When I was nine my father brought in another mother. That's what he said. Inside myself I said: No, that's a stepmother, that's different.

I was nearly expelled from my boarding school once for writing: *My stepmother is a devasting bitch* in a copybook. The nun who found it first corrected the spelling to *devastating* and then she told me quietly, little knives jumping from her eyes, to follow her to the Mistress of Studies' room. The Mistress of Studies wasn't there so the nun told me to go to the dormitory, collect my black veil and do an hour's penance in the chapel, kneeling on my bare knees with my arms outstretched, like Jesus, in front of the altar. I thumped up to the dormitory and charged back and knelt with a clattering vengeance on the chapel floor. After a while I thought 'Well at least Jesus had nails supporting his arms—and my knees hurt,' and I began to cry, but softly so the nun wouldn't hear and be proud of herself.

I remember the morning my real mother died. Our house was a very old house with tiny stairways, full of dark corners and cupboards that opened suddenly, pouring out their blackness.

The main stairs went from the hallway up to a landing where I slept, then the hallway turned past a high coloured-glass window up to another landing and flowed into a long passage. My mother's bedroom was at the end of the passage. She'd been sick for a long time. Her room was always dark and she lay very still in her bed. Strangers came in and out of our house, doctors and nurses. My mother was very yellow and when she held my hand I thought her bones were like eggshells.

It was about six o'clock one morning. I could hear the door of my mother's room opening and my father's voice calling, softly, but urgently, like electricity: 'Nurse Sheenan, Nurse Sheenan.' I crept out onto the stairs and looked up the passage. It was freezing cold and I was holding a teddy and a doll. My father saw me and put his hands to his lips and said 'Shh.' The night nurse, Nurse Sheenan, came crackling up the passage then in her stiff white apron with a navy blue cardigan over it. I went back to my room and cried and cried and held the teddy and doll and kept saying to them something like: 'Not to worry, not to worry.'

I could hear my father's heavy feet going down the stairs and him ringing the doctor, speaking very quietly in this new voice. The day nurse had just arrived and all the grown-ups were walking around and going up and down the stairs and closing the bedroom door after them. They forgot about me but I knew already.

Finally my father came in and picked me up in his arms and carried me down to my mother's room and I wasn't frightened because it wasn't my mother on the bed but a lady from a holy picture because the nurses had dressed her in a nun's habit and put rosary beads and a crucifix in her stiff yellow fingers.

All the next day people came to the house and one of the nurses gave me my lunch and she made custard that was all lumps and I began to cry then because all the people coming into the house were crying; the stairs were full of their shoes and boots going up and down, and on top, this sort of sighing and crying like a wind.

The day after my mother was buried my father sat up all night in the kitchen and drank and shouted things out into the blackness of the backyard. He broke some plates and cups and banged his fists on the kitchen table. That's when I first saw pain. I saw the madness of pain, how it bunches behind the eyes and in the throat and chest and how it must be annihilated or killed or thrown against something—killed, or it will kill you.

The next morning my father was very quiet. His chin was stuck with a piece of cotton wool where he'd cut himself shaving and his breath smelt of mouthwash. He took me away for two weeks' holiday. We stayed in a very damp hotel somewhere in the West. I never told him I'd seen him with his pain. Never talked about it, and don't even now.

My stepmother used to get me to try to talk about my real mother. She did that when she first came. I would just say, 'Oh I don't remember her at all.'

She would come in wearing her hat and her coat trimmed with imitation fur, and her high heels. She always smelt of powder. A sticky, pink smell. Even her breath smelt like that. She was always trying to kiss me then; I'd hold my breath and stiffen my back to get away from that smell.

I used to wonder how my father could share the same bedroom with her, even the same bed. I found them once in the same bed. It was a few weeks after they got married. I pretended to be sleepwalking because I wanted to get my father to come and tell me stories and put me back to bed. I came into their room and saw their bodies and the bedclothes all bunched up and the room smelled funny, musty. I bumped into a chair and my father turned round and saw me at the end of the bed and I could see his face floating and hers floating, and my father carried me back to bed but he didn't stay; he didn't even wait till I was back to sleep; he crept out and back to her and the musty bedroom.

They married the day I was nine. They had a small wedding in the local church. She was dressed in a turquoise suit and a hat with a veil over her eyes and nose. My father wore his dark pin-striped suit. I didn't speak to her the whole day and just said goodbye to my father when the taxi came to take them to the airport. They went to Majorca for two weeks. That was her idea.

It was also her idea that I go to boarding school. Right up to the day I was dispatched, with new uniform and brand new trunk, my father was quiet about it.

She said I was getting out of control, that I was with grown-ups too much or else running round on my own. She said I was more like a boy than a girl—that was to him. Once she said to one of her friends, 'She's like a little wild animal.' I heard her.

She just wanted the house to herself, and my father to herself. She was always crooking his arm and rubbing his ear and smiling cracking-powder smiles.

Everything was a smile. She'd throw out your jeans that you'd had for two summers and say, 'But they were rather old weren't they?' She'd pull at your dress at one of their damn cocktail parties (she said my father had become a terrible recluse), and she'd say, 'Tsch, tsch, Liz is such a tomboy, everything always torn.' Then she'd smile at her friends.

She didn't smile when I took two dresses her sister had sent for me from America and burnt them in the rubbish incinerator the gardener had set up in the backyard. She'd wanted to take me out in one of the dresses for Sunday lunch at one of the big hotels along the seafront.

She came and found me with bits of red taffeta and chiffon and blue nylon gently floating round the yard, a smell of burning rubber filling the garden. She screamed with rage and pulled me by the hair into my father's study holding a bit of the dress in one hand and shouting at him, her words battering his face, and he just said, 'Now, now,' and I knew then I wouldn't get punished but that she'd never forgive me either for not being the kind of daughter she wanted. She wanted someone to dress up like a doll, who would simper and trail round her friends' houses, particularly her new friends, friends of my father's.

Even when I did become a model and a doll, later, she wasn't happy; she felt I was a kind of tart or something.

I feel sorry for her now. She never had a daughter of her own and she couldn't accept me, nor me her, and my father just sat in the middle writing his books.

She was the sort of person whose accent changed completely when they were in a temper. 'Your temper will be the death of you,' she'd say to me and bang the table, and maybe I'd say nothing or maybe something like, 'Good, I'm looking forward to being dead,' and then she'd be round the table and pulling my hair and shouting, 'Ya common little hussy.'

She used to have a saying for every situation: *Once bitten, twice shy. You'll be better before you're twice married. Neither a borrower nor a lender be.* Blah blah blah. I think she must have had a book of sayings like this. I used to imagine her sitting up at night memorizing them.

After a bit I used to chant them with her; as soon as she'd said the first word, I'd know which saying it was going to be and I'd sing-song it out: '*Every cloud has a silver lining* you know dear.' She'd just look at me and then go on with whatever she was doing.

She was always doing something. Not like my father did things, slowly and carefully, word upon word of some paper for the University. No, she'd rush at things the way hens do. She'd go scatter-legged at something and knock it down and then pick it all up and start pulling at something else halfway through the first thing.

She was forever pulling at me. Before I started boarding school she pulled me into town, into tailors and hatters and cobblers. We had to go four times for fittings to the drapers who supplied the school uniform.

There were two navy serge dresses for Sundays, two mustard-coloured gymslips for every day, and two navy divided skirts for sport.

The shop smelt of deep layers of thick cloth and tweed and fluff and huge wooden counters greasy with years of polish and elbows and hands and people leaning to look at materials.

The fitters were very white-faced women in dark blue dresses. You had to stand like a rag doll while they pinched in a little bit here and a little bit there and said, 'Ach, she'll grow into it.' It was a conspiracy between them and her. It was like getting frocks from your cousins that weren't meant for you at all but just hand-me-downs and you longed for something for yourself as you were there and then.

I cried at night and thought, I'm going to boarding school because nobody here loves me.

∾ 3 ∾

Jack Hickey was the first person to whom I said, 'I love you.' We'd gone for a ride on our bikes through this new housing estate that was striding with concrete legs over the green fields of last year. Jack Hickey and I sat down on a tree trunk and he pulled out a fag and his red hair was thick and strong in the evening sun.

I said, 'I love you.' It sort of plopped out. We were both very surprised, I think, and didn't say anything else that evening. Two days before I was due to go back to school Jack Hickey asked me to go to a party with him. We danced a lot together on particularly the slow numbers and then we went outside and gave each other harsh kisses and he tried to stick his tongue into my mouth and nearly made me sick.

Jack Hickey's people were Protestants. We were Catholics. The Hickeys lived up the road. His father and mother used to shout at each other in front of the children and anyone else who used to be around and one day his little sister peed on the carpet, just took down her little nylon panties and peed and Jack Hickey's parents just laughed big cigarette laughs and went on talking.

They used to have drinks any time of the day or night, and the front door was always open; you could walk right into the parents' bedroom and see the bed unmade in the middle of the day. Jack Hickey's mother used to bathe at all times of day and then walk round with just a towel.

Protestants, I thought, are like that. Protestants are a bit funny. On Sunday not one of them got up early or put on special Sunday clothes or went to church or anything. Sunday was 'lie-in' day for the Hickeys and they wouldn't get up till midday and then they'd all cook a meal together and sit around in the afternoon reading the Sunday papers.

My stepmother said Mrs Hickey was 'a bit loud' for her taste but my father said it was nice for me to have friends. He meant Protestant friends. He wanted me to grow up non-sectarian.

When I went back to boarding school for the summer term that year I told one of the girls that I was in love with a Protestant and we were going to marry. The news went round the school in two hours. All through evening prayers there were whispers behind me and this girl passed me a note that said 'Ye'll both burn in hell fire.'

Nobody talked about anything else at school but boys. Mrs Hickey once said it was no wonder, a hundred or so girls, cooped up like that nine months out of twelve and the only male around being a decrepit and banjaxed old gardener. I thought that very daring—to even think that lack of the opposite sex would be a real problem for us.

Coming back after the holidays everyone would go through torments trying to invent boys they'd kissed, boys they'd gone on midnight walks with, boys who'd pinched and squeezed and hugged. (Everyone thought, or half thought, the other person's stories true so made up even more elaborate ones to out-tell them.) Jack Hickey was the first boyfriend I had and I was sixteen and I thought kissing was pretty awful.

The first few days of term all the older girls would be gathering into little knots in the dormitory or out on the playing fields. They'd be twisting their fingers through their hair and saying, 'God he was gaaawrgeous,' and, 'Listen, wait till I tell ya,' and they'd be describing their dresses and how they flashed a smile at him from across the room and how they had the last 'and longest and slowest dance together and… '

Then there'd be all the rules you'd have to learn. Like when he first came over to ask you to dance you'd have to get deep into conversation with the girl beside you and only answer his request for the *next dance please* after a few minutes. You'd turn and look him up and down—from under your lashes of course—and say, 'Excuse me for just a minute' to the girl you'd been talking to and swan off with him, barely touching him, barely answering his questions.

Once you'd hooked him you'd never turn up on time for a date but leave him standing by the Pillar, or outside the Stella, for at least fifteen minutes.

You wouldn't talk too much but you'd listen to him and say 'Really?' a lot and never argue.

You wouldn't let him kiss you the first time he tried; if you did he'd think you were 'easy game'. The game was anything but easy. That you learnt quickly.

Some of the girls used to sneak 'home' clothes into school. (We were supposed to come back in our uniforms and leave all our holiday gear behind.) They'd dress up at night and show us, and then the clothes would be laid out under the mattress for fear the nuns would find them and confiscate them.

Then there'd be the letters. Every morning at breakfast three girls would be appointed to hand out the letters. The more letters you got from people the more loved you were—QED. But if you got letters from boys then you were the cat's pyjamas.

The girls handing out the letters would go from table to table and everybody would be praying for a letter—any letter. Maybe a girl would pass one right by you to the girl beside you and you'd want to get up and pull her hair because she'd be torturing you, pretending there was a letter for you.

I was fighting with a girl up in the bathrooms one day and she said, 'You and your Protestant boyfriend, and he doesn't even write you a letter!' I took a bucket of water and threw it at her and most of it missed and went arcing out into the corridor and the nun came in and sent me to bed without any supper.

One girl was found writing passionate love letters to herself. She was taken away from school by her parents that week. We all said, 'God, the poor thing' and thanked God it wasn't us because all of us had planned the same thing many a time.

Boys and clothes and pimples and Evelyn Home were a tide you couldn't swim against. Your best friend would start getting letters and go all dreamy and say 'Tom, oh Tom' in the middle of the night, pretending she was asleep, and you'd be half laughing at her and half embarrassed.

But she'd have a picture of him in her prayer book and make up poems to him and cut out pictures of clothes from fashion magazines and write 'Mrs Tom O'Hara' in her copybook and push it over to you saying, 'How do you think it looks?'

Finally I decided. I sat up one night under the bedclothes with a torch and wrote a letter to Jack Hickey. I said I was having a grand time and how was he. I said I hoped his parents were well and his little sister. I said we were just about to go into our Annual Retreat, and then crossed that out as he wouldn't know what it meant, being a Protestant. I said, 'It would be lovely to get a letter from you if you had a mo. Bye for now, Liz.'

In the morning the letter looked rather forlorn and silly but I gave it to one of the day-girls anyway with a bar of chocolate if she'd post it and keep her mouth buttoned. She couldn't have told anyone anyway without committing a sin. The next day we were going into our Annual Retreat.

The Annual Retreat was when all of us, nuns and pupils, kept silent for three whole days and three whole nights. We kept silent in order to contemplate, meditate, think about our past sins and make resolutions (usually impossible ones) for the future. We were supposed to think about God and sin and the devil and the saints. We didn't have any classes and we all went round trying to look very solemn and holy.

In fact, during retreats we all went mad on sex. You couldn't think about anything else. We'd be in a turmoil reading the holy books the nuns gave us to uplift our minds and trying to glean information on the forbidden subject from the *Legion of Mary Handbook for Young Ladies.*

Priests would come in from outside Orders to give us the retreat. A different priest every year. We'd have talks from them in the school chapel about four times a day and then confessions and rosary and Mass and Benediction and night devotions. A veritable orgy of religion.

One priest who came was called Father Moriarty and he was from Limerick and he used to sail on the Shannon with his rich parishioners. He was young and tanned and all the girls were dying with love for Father Moriarty.

Father Moriarty was all for modern Catholicism. He had all the nuns in a flat spin when he asked for a blackboard and chalk to be brought into the chapel. *In the chapel Sister!* Then he came sweeping in for his evening talk. The evening talks were just for the senior girls and they were always to do with sex.

Well this evening Father Moriarty came in and whipped off his black soutane and stood there under the sacristy light in white shirt and black trousers and said, 'Tonight I'm going to discuss some of the problems attached to the sexual act. First VD.' I thought VD meant Veni Domine, Lord come, like in the hymn books, but there was a great shhing in the chapel and every girl was convinced that Father Moriarty was talking directly to her and we followed his every word and complex diagrams with intense concentration.

Valerie was the envy of the whole school because she asked for a 'special talk' with Father Moriarty as she had 'A Problem'. He'd said he would be available to each and all of us during the entire retreat period. Valerie was taken down to his room while he was having breakfast. She said two sisters from the kitchen waited on him the whole time and the breakfast he got would have fed eight of us—porridge and cream, bacon and eggs and toast—and he told her, 'Help yourself,' and handed her his side plate but her hands were shaking so much that she dropped the egg in the sugar bowl and he laughed and said, 'Not to worry,' and pinched her cheek and she nearly fainted, she said.

Valerie had wanted to know if French kissing was a sin. A mortal sin. (Mortal sins meant you went to hell and burnt and burnt for ever and ever.) Father Moriarty had told us that you could get this VD thing from kissing and everyone was terrified and thinking: When did I last kiss a boy?

Was French kissing a mortal sin or not? Valerie in her excitement couldn't quite remember. The priest had said it depended on what it meant in the whole context of the relationship, and she didn't know what context meant. We told her it meant the whole works, the situation. The priest said it might lead to sinning, it might lead to all sorts of things, but it wasn't necessarily a sin on its own.

The next day I waited for an hour to go to confession. Most of us went to confession at least twice a day that retreat. We'd be kneeling in the chapel benches and no one would dare sit up and some of the girls would be crying and pushing their rosary beads round and round and saying 'Oh God' under their breath so's you knew they were *grappling with a terrible moral problem*. The longer you stayed in the confessional the higher your credit rating went.

I got up to go into the confession box and the missal fell out of my hands and holy pictures scattered and I gave a little 'Oh' and the priest opened his green curtain and looked out and said, 'Take your time,' and the pictures were sticking to my hands and I couldn't get a grip on them, and I was sweating because it was a terrible thing for a priest to see your face before you went into confession; they were never supposed to know who told them what sins. One of the nuns once told us a story of a French priest who died at the scaffold rather than tell somebody's sins.

I put my lips right up near the grill and started whispering, 'Bless me, Father, for I have sinned . . .' and then I nearly dropped out of my standing because his two eyes were wide open and looking back at me, and usually the priest would just turn his ear to the black grill and you'd pour your sins through to him, like molasses into a funnel.

Father Moriarty just smiled and said, 'Okay now, have you any problems?' He didn't want to hear the sins at all. Just problems. So I told him about Jack Hickey, about him being a Protestant and the way he pushed his tongue in and asked, 'Was that French kissing, Father?'

He said, 'It could be the start of French kissing.'

'Was it sinful?'

Then he said, 'Did you feel his thing stiffening up against you as he kissed you?'

'Whaaat?' I said, nervous.

'His penis,' he said. 'Did you feel it stiffening up when he kissed you?'

And I got up and ran out of the box and down the chapel, the tears pouring down my face and it was the talk of the school for days. Everyone thought I'd done some really terrible sin.

∽ 4 ∽

There was a rule in school you learned to live by. The rule was: You live by, for, and through your emotions. School was weeping over boys, and crying at the Stations of the Cross for poor Jesus hanging up between the thieves. School was begging God to forgive the sins of the whole world if you gave up Marietta biscuits for a whole week and wore your vest every day. School was falling madly in love with other girls and falling out again with a white face, red eyes and loss of appetite. School was standing on your bed trying to have a look at your legs in the six-inch mirror and doing novenas to Saint Theresa to make them look like Marlene Dietrich's. School was hearing of President Kennedy's death and howling your eyes out and trying to get a look at Paris Match and the blood on Jackie Kennedy's costume and saying, 'God, how *AWWWful*' and never asking why was it done but just sloshing around in the gasps and gawps of a street crowd at a car accident.

School was a continuation of, and a preparation for, our future—the future of nice middle class ladies who, having had hundreds of pounds spent on their education, would never be expected to do anything except marry, or maybe become a nun, but hardly have a career. Hardly.

Everyone accepted that somebody like Geraldine Doyle might have a career. She was odd. She was very good at maths and washed her hair with detergent and played the cello. She killed herself last year. She was found in her flat having spent two years teaching maths in a girls' secondary school. She put her head, detergent-washed hair and all, in the gas oven, and turned it on.

Our last year at school we were allowed to wear our home clothes on weekends and school holidays.

The first night back after the holidays we'd all be up in the dormitory, our cases balanced up on our beds, our cubicle curtains drawn back and our clothes laid out.

Valerie came in wearing knee-high leather boots, and everything you had then looked tatty and worn out and you wanted to kill your parents for only letting you take what you had taken. She let me try the boots on and I stroked the soft leather against my legs and wanted the boots so much that it hurt like a knife twisting inside. That's what it was then the whole time: I want, want, want—at night in bed thinking about the other girls' clothes; wondering what they'd all wear next weekend; pleased to think that Margaret Daly looked a right eejit in a long kilt and white blouse and wondering how Elaine Mullen always looked so neat; squeezing the cheeks of your bottom together in bed to stiffen it and make it look pert like Hayley Mills'. Lying so tense and wondering, whispers like bats over the partition walls: *Mary ... are you awake? Listen, wait till I tell ya...*

The first Sunday back that term somebody spilt nail varnish over Valerie's angora twin set. The girl, Margaret Daly, cried out like she'd been stabbed and was mopping at the nail varnish like it was a bleeding wound. Valerie took the twin set and tossed it into a corner. 'I'll send it home to Mammy for one of the kids,' she said.

God I'd love it, you thought, tarnished and all.

But you wouldn't say that. Sit mum and pretend that it was the only thing in the world to do with angora twin sets that had nail varnish on them.

We'd spent the whole of that morning up in the dormitory, swapping clothes with smiles, and jumping in and out of each other's cubicles and envying and wanting so that the air was electric blue and we were all laughing and saying how grand the other one looked, and how that little jumper looks far better on you than it does on me and not meaning a word of it.

Friendships that year became very fragile, brittle things. Everyone wanted Valerie to be her friend. Valerie was the apex, the pinnacle of our desires. Valerie had long legs and Valerie had masses of boyfriends—none of whom she gave a damn for; Valerie was as good as gold in class and all the teachers thought she was adorable and Valerie wrote poems about the teachers after class and passed them round her friends. They would have made the teachers' hair go quite white.

The juniors would send Valerie letters. *Valerie, I love you.* She'd show them to her cronies at recreation and everyone would laugh and roll about and put their hands to their mouths, keeping an eye on Valerie at the same time.

That was the same term we had the woman from the Dorothy Grey cosmetics group come and give us a talk on how to make ladies of ourselves.

She was terribly slim, like a doll, and wore a light green wool top and matching skirt. She spoke so carefully that the tip of her nose moved with her lips.

She said it was a woman's duty, her responsibility, to make the very best of herself. She said that nobody liked an ugly woman, a fat woman, a spotty woman. She said there was no need to be any of these things—with constant care and attention every woman could look attractive.

She said we must regard our faces as blank boards and etch in our beauty like an artist does a painting.

I thought of us all etching and scratching and squeezing for the rest of our lives. A long time.

She told us the kind of things a woman must *never* do in front of her husband. (Valerie said, 'What about in front of her lover?' but so quietly only those of us near her caught it. We giggled: *Lovers indeed.*) The cosmetic lady said a woman must never pluck her eyebrows, or cut her toenails, or shave her legs, in her husband's presence.

One of the vulgar day-girls said, 'What about picking her nose?'

For a minute a wave nearly engulfed us all; we were hanging on the edge of a swinging, tumultuous cliff, but the cosmetic lady gave a brief, flicking smile like a snake's tongue in the girl's direction, and carried on.

We sat on the edges of our chairs, listening and twisting our hair round our fingers and wanting and promising ourselves with fierce promises that we would be beautiful and we wouldn't ever cut our toenails or shave our legs in front of our husbands. Not ever.

The cosmetic lady tried to persuade the nuns to take some samples of goods for us but the nuns said: No thank you.

Enough was enough.

We could never have enough of husbands and along with husbands came babies. We were all going to have babies. If anyone's parents came visiting to the school with one of the girls' baby brothers or baby sisters, we would all stand around and say, 'Ahh, the little dote.' But really husbands were more important than babies. Anyone could have babies—you had to work to have a husband. Somebody told us that in Dublin there were three girls for every one man and we thought, 'Jesus!'

On a little shelf outside the chapel at school there was a box for Black Babies. If you gave the nun in charge of chapel half-a-crown then you 'bought' yourself a Black Baby. I bought one and I called her Josephine Agnes. You could call them anything you liked as long as the name was a saint's name. Then the nun would write up your name and the baby's name: *Elizabeth O'Sullivan* (in the nuns' italic handwriting) has adopted (in print) *Baby Josephine Agnes* (written in the nuns' slanting hand again). Your half-a-crown was sent to the missions in Africa and the nuns there called one of their new converts Josephine Agnes. Babies were that simple.

Josephine was the name of Napoleon's wife and at home in my father's study I'd read a book about her. She was rather daring but the history teacher just went on and on about Napoleon and batons in people's haversacks and dates of battles that you couldn't remember. I tried to tell her about the book on Josephine and she just said, 'My dear child, I think you will find you have quite enough to do without frittering away your time reading irrelevant books on obscure females in history.' She said, 'Mmm' when I couldn't remember the dates again.

Another female in our history was Marie Antoinette. She was very beautiful and the horrible revolutionaries chopped her head off, but at least she'd been able to say, 'Let them eat cake' when the people of Paris were starving for lack of a piece of bread. We thought that was marvellous.

We also thought Africa was marvellous. We learnt a bit about it in history; that's why we adopted Black Babies, because we knew they were having a terrible time out in the jungle being pagans and everything, and white men went out to 'darkest' Africa and helped the 'natives' and the 'savages', and we had a picture in our history reader of how they got put in big stewing pots for their pains, and black fellows with very long legs and mad eyes danced around them. The white ones kept their hard hats on even in the stewpots.

A nun from one of the missions made a visit to the school one day and we all vowed we'd go to Africa. I was going to go and work in a leper colony and I asked the nurse to let me work in the school infirmary so's I'd get used to looking at horrible deformities, but there was only gravel in people's knees, and cold sores on people's lips.

I imagined myself slim, green-eyed and white-coated with a stethoscope round my neck, the lepers holding out their stumps of limbs in grateful praise as I walked amongst them. There'd be a lone (young, tanned, handsome, intelligent, etc. etc.) priest there also, and we'd altruistically give up our lives and fight the jungle and the disease and the devil together.

I'd pinch myself at night in bed to see how much pain I could stand, because you'd have to be like iron to take Africa. I'd lie on the lino floor with my nightie off and clamp my mouth to stop my teeth chattering and think: If I died now how tragic it would be...

I'd imagine all the girls round my bed, my body laid out, a little smile on my dead face. All the girls would be weeping and Valerie would be crying loudest and throwing herself across my body. My father and stepmother would be led in by one of the nuns and she'd stand back and my father would have big tears pouring down his face, and he'd pick me up and push past my stepmother, saying in a choked voice, 'Oh Lizzie, my little child, I've come to take you home for the last time,' and then the girls would really shriek with crying and a big sobbing procession would go down through the town to the train bound for Dublin.

✑ 5 ✑

At school we were the Nice Girls.

Nice Girls didn't do things like that, or that.

Nice Girls didn't swear or dog-ear their copybooks or write 'Dev is a Pig' on their history readers.

Nice Girls always cleaned their nails before Mass and their teeth before sleep and ate up all their green veg—even leeks and cabbage. Nice Girls *never* whistled, nor did they sing or shout at the top of their voices even if they were at the far end of the hockey field.

Nice Girls didn't run down the school corridors, or skid round corners or roll the sleeves of their blouses up or the tops of their knee socks down. Nice girls always curtsied to the head nun, offered to carry the teachers' books and stood back, flat against the wall, when a group of nuns and visitors passed by.

Nice Girls kept their uniforms and their bodies without blemish and their desks in the study room exquisitely tidy. Nice Girls didn't argue with the teachers or the nuns—even if the latter happened to assert that the sun spun continuously round the earth. Nice Girls didn't tell tales but they always owned up if they'd done something wrong and even offered to clean up other people's wrongs—if they were really nice girls.

If Nice Girls were asked what they wanted to be by grownups they'd say, 'The Mother of a Family,' as if it were a religion; if they were asked by nuns, they'd say, 'A nun.'

Nice Girls were unobtrusive. A Nice Girl didn't smell or raise her voice, or argue, or fight, or hit people over the head for calling her father a Blueshirt.

Nice Girls gave up all sport once they were sixteen except some polite tennis. They also gave up science and took up domestic because the science teacher had brought in a rabbit for dissection, and Nice Girls cried and tried to make themselves sick in the lav and had to be calmed down by the school nurse.

Nice Girls kept diaries and made resolutions which they used to cry over, and all went into town to the funeral of the history teacher when she died even though they'd made her life a living hell, and they all screwed up their tiny handkerchiefs into little balls and the women in the town thought they looked awfully pathetic and sweet.

Nice Girls were the first into bras, the first to wear deodorants, the first to wear nylons, and the first to start washing their knickers every night and sleeping in them to make them dry for the morning.

Nice Girls wept when they read *Little Women*, and their reading careers stopped there.

Nice Girls talked about boys most of the time and how to hook, hoodwink, capture, delight, enslave and enthrall members of that curious race.

We were all supposed to be Nice Girls.

∽ **6** ∽

Every Saturday and Sunday we had what was known as 'The Parlour'. That is, between the hours of 2.00 p.m. on Saturday and 6.00 p.m. on Sunday, the girls of St Margaret's Boarding School were available for visits.

Not just anyone was allowed to visit—only parents, aged relatives, and friends from religious orders, i.e. nuns or priests. The relatives had to be old, otherwise you could have boyfriends turning up on Saturday or Sunday saying, 'I'm Miss O'Brien's first cousin and I'd like to take her out for the day.' Oh, anything could have happened. So, the relatives had to be old. Presumably old ones wouldn't try anything.

One Sunday I was reading a novel about the French Revolution. The study room looked as if it were smoking, with gentle streams of sunlight dropped through the high windows. The man in the novel was being taken on the back of a tumbril to have his aristocratic head severed from his neck, but he was going to escape; you didn't know how.

The sister's hand on my shoulder made me jump. 'You're wanted in the Parlour,' she whispered, that special nun whisper that would carry for miles.

I walked up the study behind the sister. (The sisters worked in the kitchen and on the farm and at reception. They were the country girls, the poor ones, whose fathers couldn't afford big dowries or expensive educations, so they just crept into the religious orders and looked after the other nuns, the rich ones. The rich nuns were called 'Ma'am' and they did the teaching.)

Once I got out of the study I belted up to the dormitory and flick-brushed my hair and scrabbled through my locker for the one pair of tights Mary (which is what I now call my stepmother as Valerie said it is more sophisticated) had bought me before coming back. They were smelly so I flung them back, did a quick lick over the eyebrows like some actress in some film, and then I was running back down the stairs, down the long corridors, skidding round the corners, not stopping for nuns or anyone and feeling the 'Tschs' and the sighs following me, catching in my way like little twigs when you're running through a forest, today not minding them, and coming to the door of the Parlour and suddenly stopping – thinking, Who can it be? Nobody ever comes to visit me in the Parlour.

I was thinking, I'll go back and find the sister and ask her to describe the visitor to me, when the door of the Parlour swung open and the nun smiled—'Ah! Here she is!' I stood there feeling stripped naked, the faces smiling before me.

They were the Hickeys. Mr and Mrs and Jack. Mrs Hickey was smoking and laughing at something the nun had said. The smoke was filling the tiny room with its polished table, parquet floor, overstuffed armchairs (with linen doilies on the arms and back to stop the upholstery getting soiled), *The Messenger* and

The Life of St Theresa on the table and a bowl of flowers—waxy-looking flowers.

'Hello then Lizzie,' Mrs Hickey said. I cleared my throat and said, 'Hello.'

'So,' Mrs Hickey said, pleased with herself, her smoke billowing round her, 'So where, Sister, do you think would be the best place to go?' You could see the nun wincing. She was supposed to be called 'Ma'am'. She'd surely take it out on me later.

Mrs Hickey didn't seem to notice. The nun looked smaller, paler, under the bright battery of questions.

'The Abbey ruins are said to make a nice trip,' said the nun. (She had to say, 'are said to', because the nuns never went out, so she was just passing on advice she'd been given by some other visitors.)

'Oh ruins indeed,' said Mrs Hickey with a bouncing laugh, and you thought the nun might crack in two under the weight and sharpness of it. She pressed her lips together. Her hands were under her habit, clenching. You felt sure they must have been clenching.

Outside the sun was so bright. You felt like a worm coming out from under a stone, soft and white.

Jack was wearing his cricket whites and a purple blazer. They'd picked him up at his school on the way down. He said hello, but looked cross and scuffed pebbles as you walked to the car.

You wondered, So will it always be like this? One week they say, 'I love you', and there are kisses and odd rushing feelings, then a month later there's a silence, a coldness, and they don't look at you. It's like being a child again. You thought being sixteen would be so much better. One minute they pat you on the head, they laugh at you, they say, 'Oh now, listen to the funny child.' Then their faces go sour, like old green apples. They say, 'Oh get along with you now, off you go to the nursery,' or, 'Off you go to bed.' You think, Perhaps men will be like parents: difficult to please, difficult to understand, difficult to follow because they're busy or talking to someone or just about to dash off to the College, darling. Yes. You think men are bound to be like that.

'It's so bloody antediluvian, Char,' Mrs Hickey was saying, linking her husband's arm; the two of them were laughing, but he said, 'Wait till we get out of earshot, Vera.' You felt a bit of a fool. Being in a place they thought so odd.

We got into their car. An old Peugeot saloon with brown leather seats, the upholstery done like thick sausages. It was like their house, full of old Sunday papers and empty bottles and cigarette packs squashed flat.

Jack and I sat in the back. We were careful not to touch each other. He looked out the window and whistled through his teeth. Mr Hickey said, 'Why don't we go and knock up old Foster for a couple of jars?' and Mrs Hickey said, 'Why not?' and she lit up more cigarettes and offered us one. I said, 'I don't indulge thanks' and Mrs Hickey thought that was the funniest thing she'd ever heard, and I laughed a bit, just to be polite; it's always difficult to laugh so much when you've started the joke. Jack smoked.

Jack said, 'Thanks for your letter.' I said, 'Oh not at all, it was just for something to do really.' I thought, Sweet Jesus let him keep his voice down. I could hear Mrs Hickey's laugh. 'Oh love letters is it?'

Jack just went on looking out of the window. So, I thought, no more letters.

Then Mr Hickey turned on the radio. It was Top of the Pops. Jack and I hummed the tunes, looking out the windows. He laughed; he said I'd got the words wrong, but at least it was better than trying to talk. Every time we went round corners I could see him without turning my head round and actually staring.

The part of the country we were driving through was very nice. It was full of small lakes, grey ones with reeds like little crowds round the edges, bending. It had boggy ground and rivers connecting the lakes so the road seemed a very definite sort of hardness and blackness in the midst of the bogs and the wetness. The country is quite flat and if you go very fast it looks like streaming greens and browns—soft. But if you go slowly you can see all the holes and hillocks and bits of rock barely covered with moss and different grasses and then it's a wild endless rug of colours and textures.

The Fosters, who we are going to see, are Protestants like the Hickeys. They're the same Protestants who came to Ireland in the sixteenth and seventeenth centuries and were given, or 'bought up' (they paid almost nothing) huge tracts of land, the best land in the soft green heart of the country. Some were given the land as a reward for fighting the King of England's wars, or the Queen of England's—something like that. The Irish peasants were shoved out to boggy land where they could only grow spuds and scratch around for a living. The Irish were always fighting each other so they never got time to get organized and fight the English off their land.

At school we had three main things against Protestants. They had taken the land off our ancestors; they didn't believe that the Virgin Mary was God's mother or in the miracles at Lourdes or anything else for that matter; and they weren't Catholics.

My father knew a lot of Protestants because most of the other professors and lecturers at his University were Protestants and it was even supposed to be a mortal sin for Catholics to go to his University, though many of them did anyway.

I once asked my father if it was true that all Protestants would burn in hell and he said, 'Ah go on with all that rubbish, who's telling ye that?' I was sent out of history class for a whole week then because I said my father had told me that blaming the Prods for everything, and saying they'd burn in hell, was a lot of rubbish.

The Fosters were rich Protestants. They had a big farm and then a business in Dublin as well. Mr Foster was always flying to London for working trips. He'd fly to London on business the way most people would take a bus from Sandymount to town. He used to come and visit my father sometimes when he was in Dublin and they'd take the bottle of port or wine into my father's study and talk about the times when the Protestants had all the big country houses. Mr Foster was a sort of amateur historian on Protestant history in Ireland.

The Fosters' house is an old Georgian one. Its left wing is completely covered in Virginia Creeper that moves like a lake the whole time, whispering. Inside there are long stone passages where the centre is worn down from thousands and thousands of footsteps of maids and manservants and butlers walking, running, scurrying, to answer the bell-pull of the lord and lady of the manor. There are huge fireplaces where you put logs the size of six-year-old children and they don't stick out.

The house is full of smells and sighs and echoes. There are rooms that are quite empty. There's one room where the boards groan as you walk in and a wooden rocking horse stands in the centre. The Fosters spend most of their time in the drawing room. The rest of the rooms huddle around with their memories. Once there were tutors, and governesses, and children exploring, and aunts.

Mary, my stepmother, my father and I once visited the Fosters on a Sunday. Mary said, 'For heaven's sake, why don't you get in some central heating, let off the east wing during the summer and get fitted carpets for the bedrooms you use and the lounge?' The Fosters looked at her and nobody said anything. Mrs Foster looked as if she'd been asked: Why don't you buy yourself a nice see-through blouse and miniskirt instead of that old tweed suit? But nobody said anything. Mr Foster went Hmph, and sort of grinned and said to his wife, 'Well now, what about another cup of tea, uh?'

Today anyway we drove up the long avenue, the trees nudging each other as we passed by.

Mr Foster appeared in the hall door and about five dogs came barking and jumping over the gravel. The Hickeys shook his hand and then Mrs Hickey drew me forward and said, 'This is Miles O'Sullivan's daughter, you remember her of course?' Mr Foster put a hand on each of my shoulders and said, 'My, my.' He didn't say, 'How you've grown,' but it was the same thing, the way he looked and was surprised.

It was only then that I realized I was still in my navy blue school uniform. Socks too, and oh, I wished for the tights even though they had been a bit smelly. I wanted to be gone, away, dead. Jack looked so casual in his cricket gear—damn men, it was always easier for them, always.

Mr Foster kept saying, 'Well now, what a nice surprise,' and he walked into the house and we all followed and he shouted for his wife: 'Visitors, darling.'

Mrs Foster is like a hungry cat. She's so thin and nervy. She dives at words and people and conversations as if they were the first and last she'd ever get. She was wearing this sort of long dress which Valerie told me later was a housecoat.

'Come in, come in,' she said with a screeching smile on her face. She darted at each one of us and then darted at the door and shrieked, 'Dora! Bring four more cups.'

'Vera, how *are* you?' she said to Mrs Hickey, her head on one side like a thrush. She said it as if she expected something awful to have happened to Mrs Hickey.

Mrs Hickey was saying, 'Oh fine thanks' and fishing in her bag for her lighter and trying to catch Mr Hickey's eye so he'd get her a light.

Mrs Foster jumped up ('Oh how stupid of me') and she turned to her son who was watching everything with the amused, and I thought entirely faked, tolerance of a twenty-year-old.

The son was called Alec. He was reading History and Philosophy at Trinity. Before that he'd been educated at a public school in England. He seemed the epitome of education and sophistication and maleness. Everything we as 'Nice Girls' had been told to long and look for. Jack suddenly looked gauche and awkward. The Protestants in England give themselves a much better education, I thought to myself.

Alec nodded as we were introduced and his hair slid forward on his forehead as he did so, so he had to flip his head back. You knew he'd practised that.

Mrs Foster stood for a minute, perplexed, almost as if she'd forgotten who she was. Then she said, 'Ah yes, and this is Pepita,' and her hand fluttered towards Pepita. Pepita was Alec's girlfriend and she was also at Trinity, reading English Lit. She said, 'Helleow' and smiled without opening her lips. I thought she was beautiful—all legs, like a foal. She had her legs curled up under her and she made the battered old armchair look comfortable, attractive. She was one of those kinds of people.

'What'll we all have to drink then?' Mr Foster shouted, and stood by the sideboard, rubbing his hands like a butcher. The Hickeys said they'd have gin and tonics, and Jack said he'd have a beer, and I said a gin and tonic because I'd had one before at a wedding. The others already had drinks. We all got big thick glasses full of gin and tonic and the ice clinked, and the drinks sparkled blue.

Pepita said, 'Would you like some music?' to nobody in particular, and walked over to the record player and sank down onto her knees and slicked her index finger over the record sleeves. I thought she looked like a little child; she did everything so gently, so humbly, people must have wanted to protect her, particularly men. She put on a John McCormack record and his thick voice filled the room: 'Drink to me only with thine eyes …'

I thought of an article I'd read somewhere about what prisoners feel like during their first week or so out of prison; how apart and different and somehow undefined they think they are. That's how I felt out of boarding school. I thought if my head were shaved it would make no difference. Everyone else seemed so sure of themselves. They talked, laughed, made jokes, chose records, just walked about the room. You felt yourself to be all corners and your words came out heavy and blunt like unrisen bread. The older ones, particularly the older women, ones like Pepita, they'd always look better, you thought, always look at ease.

Dora, this very cross maid, came in, and then banged out, with the tea things. Little cucumber sandwiches, cakes, shortbread—you'd almost die for one of them when you got back to school but everyone else seemed so disinterested; you were determined not to be different. At least as little different as possible. Not to fall on the plate and gobble them and run out to the garden like a dog does and finish them all up, nervously looking over your shoulder.

The gin was beginning to give me a tight feeling above the bridge of my nose; my eyes felt bulgy and slightly sensitive.

Alec said, 'Would you like to go and look at the horses?' and got up to walk out.

I said, 'Oh yes' and jumped up because I'd been dying to see the horses all afternoon but you couldn't ask. I knocked over Mrs

Hickey's glass of gin and somebody said, 'Aha, tiddly again,' and Mrs Foster shouted 'Dora!' and I just stood looking at the gin on the carpet and Mrs Hickey smiled and patted my hand and Alec said, 'Oh come on. Who cares about the bloody carpet?'

Alec, Jack and I walked out into the sunlight across the cobbled yard to the stables. Pepita stayed behind.

I had cousins in Dublin who had horses and last summer I'd gone over to their house quite a lot at weekends and we used to go riding in the park in the evening and the cold air would be like hands pulling at your cheeks, pony hooves stamping a cross pattern on the ground; your body and your mind would be like a streamer, all in one concentration of movement.

The Fosters had six horses and two ponies. Two of the horses they didn't own but just stabled for this English businessman who used to come over and hunt during the Irish hunting season.

We looked into each loose box and the horses shuffled around and blew down their noses at us and twitched their ears, and the groom called Alec 'Master Alec' and wore old-fashioned riding breeches and leather leggings, polished like a stone in a brown pool. Ancient.

Alec asked if we'd like to go for a ride; Jack said he didn't mind and I said I'd love to. So Alec said to the groom, 'Bailey, saddle up the mare and the gelding will you?' and went off to get me a pair of his sister's jodhpurs.

Alec took a big strong bay horse, Jack took Alec's roan gelding and I took his sister's Connemara mare. The mare was cream with a deep brown-black mane and tail. We rode out under the arch, across the paddock and then swung down along the avenue. Alec was very casual, twisting round in his saddle, the reins in one hand his other hand resting on his horse's broad hindquarters; Jack was very stiff, holding the reins high; I could feel the mare's warmth beneath me and her delicate stepping and I thought, May this go on for ever and ever.

That year we were having an Indian summer. It was late September and the sun still had a golden softening warmth in it. The slanting winds and rain hadn't begun yet.

Alec broke into a trot and then a canter and the mare pricked her ears forward and followed and I could see Jack still stiff and bumping along, his horse uncomfortable. Then we were galloping, the horses exciting each other, and you were in control and yet not in control, and you tore the air apart in front of you like ripping silk.

I turned round just in time to see Jack careering over his horse's head. He'd put the horse at a fallen tree; the horse just stopped dead in front of it, and Jack carried on and landed on the ground like a bag of potatoes. 'Damn and bloody damn' said Jack and you wanted to laugh but didn't. He was brushing the leaves off and there was a bright green stain down his cricket whites, like green blood.

Jack said he'd had enough. He said he was going to walk back to the house and he'd see us there later. He climbed back up on his horse again and then Alec shouted, 'Okay, c'mon,' to me and we galloped off away into the wet reds and browns of the Foster woods.

We stopped finally by an old gate lodge at the edge of the woods. There was a river running below. The lodge was covered in ivy, the windows under fronds of greenery, buried like a Yorkshire terrier's eyes.

'Why don't we get down?' Alec said. 'Come and have a look inside. It's my sort of private den since I was a kid.'

I got down. My legs felt funny, the ground swaying slightly. I hadn't ridden for weeks. We looped the horses' reins over a gatepost. Alec said, 'They won't go away.'

Alec opened the door, pushing it back stiffly. 'As the spider said to the fly, "Won't you come into my parlour?"' he said, and stood back and I went in.

It was very dark inside; the ivy kept the light out. A dark, dank smell. In one corner was an old sofa, the other a desk, then an old record player, some books, a kitchen dresser.

Alec banged down into the sofa. 'Whaddya think of it?' he said. 'Mmm, it's lovely,' I said. 'It must have been very nice to have somewhere to be on your own when you were a child.' It sounded prim even as I said it. He laughed. 'Even better now.' He had one arm along the back of the sofa. 'Come along then, sit down, relax.' He said the words like orders. I knew I was going to sit down. I felt powerless suddenly, goggle-eyed, like a rabbit in front of a ferret.

I didn't dare look at Alec. I wished I'd never come in here. I sat on the edge of the sofa without letting my back touch the sofa back where Alec's hand lay.

'I'm not going to eat you, you know,' Alec said, and he laughed a smug laugh.

'I know,' I said. I know, I thought. I know he's going to try it.

I don't want it. Yet I do. It's some sort of recognition, isn't it? But I'm scared. It will be something to tell them at school. But I'm scared. I want to go back.

'Don't you think we'd better go back?' I said. I thought: For God's sake, my voice sounds ludicrous.

'No hurry,' said Alec. 'No hurry at all.' He brought his hand down from the back of the sofa. Started tickling the back of my neck. Then stretching his fingers up through my hair so I got goose pimples all over. Then he jerked round and pushed me back against the sofa and I could feel his face and his hair in my eyes and his teeth were hurting my lip and his hands were scrabbling in my clothes and he was saying, or sort of groaning, 'Hold me, hold me' and he jammed his knee up between my legs and then I just bit his tongue as hard as I could.

'You little—' He jumped up and stood looking at me and was yelling, 'You bloody little Catholic virgin!' and he was panting and I thought, He's going to punch me, really punch me in the face, but he just stood there: 'Rubbish ... schoolgirl ... virgin ... whore ... kid...' and he was shouting the words and I thought he looked ugly and cruel and I felt awful and yet I felt: Well it's better than that ... but than what?

Alec slammed outside and took a few mouthfuls of water from the river and flattened his hair down and I came out after him, very quiet, and I got back up onto the mare.

We rode back to the house. All the warmth and strength seemed to have left the sky. It seemed the colours were stretched thinly, the sky itself deflated like an old polythene bag.

Alec said nothing. He didn't ask me not to tell anyone what

had happened. He didn't have to. He knew I'd failed, not him. There were certain rules. If you broke them you took the broken pieces away with you and they clattered around inside your head: Fraud … fraud… fraud.

✑ 7 ✑

The nuns said: 'Your body is the temple of the Holy Ghost, the Third Person of the Blessed Trinity. You must always therefore treat it with loving respect.'

The woman from Dorothy Grey said: 'You must regard your face as a blank board and etch in beauty like an artist … everyone can be beautiful.'

The nuns said: 'Your body is the source of many temptations to sin. Your mouth can eat too much and drink too much; your eyes can see, read, watch, evil things; your hands can make mischief: idle hands for the devil's work; your legs can lead you into occasions of mortal sin …'

The song said: 'My face is my fortune, sir.'

The girl in the magazine said: 'You too can have a body like mine if you use this super lotion'; 'Watch out for the New You when you wear Sparklelight'; 'Make yourself this fabulous sexy dress'.

The nuns said: 'The love between a man and his wife is a very beautiful thing. But sex. Sex is dirty. Sex is sinful. Sex is spitting in the face of God … Girls, the switching off of the ignition key can be the start of a mortal sin. Girls, girls, we must always be chaste, pure …'

The young girl in the love comic said: 'His first kiss sent a quivering passion through my body. I could feel the texture of his hands, strong yet bony, through the thin stuff of my dress … I thought he must hear my heart pounding—to me it sounded like the thunder of the gods …'

The nuns said: 'God made you. God loves you. God will forgive you. God has punished you. God is watching you. God is testing you.'

The magazine said: 'Test whether you are REALLY IN LOVE' (it gave you twenty questions to fill in with a choice of three each time). 'Do you feel your heart skipping a beat whenever you hear his name mentioned? Do you blush constantly? Would you mind if your best friend told you she'd been asked by him to go to a party? Have you lost your appetite?'

The nuns said: 'Come along then, eat up, otherwise you won't grow up to be a big, strong girl.'

The book said: 'Today's girl is tall and slim; she moves with the sleek elegance of the greyhound and the casual grace of the wild animal.'

The nuns said: 'If it weren't for our souls we'd be just like wild animals.'

The comic said: 'They ran into the bedroom and fell on each other like animals …'

The nuns said: 'We want you to grow up to be the handmaids of Christ.'

The magazine said: 'It is still every young girl's dream to grow up and be the mother of a family. It's the most natural thing in the world.'

The boy said: 'I want to grow up and be a soldier, and boss people around, like my Dad does.'

The girl said: 'When I grow up I'm going to have a house with three bedrooms, and twenty dresses, and a husband as rich as rich as …'

The girl in the film said: 'More than anything else in the world I want to be your wife. I want to give you my whole self … my all …'

The hymn said: 'All I have I give Thee, give Thyself to me …'

The song said: 'All you need is love, love, love. Love is all you need.'

The advertisement said: 'Feeling depressed? What you need is a course of these revolutionary, new, extra, extra strong vitamin tablets.'

Your stepmother said: 'What you need is a haircut and some new clothes.'

The nuns said: 'What you need is the strong hand of discipline all your life.'

Your father said: 'I'm sure I don't know what you need.'

The advertisements said: 'You need this and that and the other and then you'll be different, younger, sexier, sleeker, thinner, fatter, glossier, posher …'

The man in the comic said to the bookish girl: 'What you need, my dear girl, is a man.'

You said: 'What I need … is … is …'

So it goes on.

∽ 8 ∽

My second last term at school I fell in love. The girl was called Ann. She was from Mullingar. She was called Ann because her father had wanted a boy and was going to call him Dan. When a girl arrived they called her Ann. A compensation.

Ann's father was a big cattle farmer. She had two brothers and five sisters. They used to all come and visit her; the father red-faced and always looking angry, though it may have been fear that made him look like that. The children sat in the back of the big black Mercedes and looked out. Ann's father was in with all the big Fianna Fáil men in the country. That's how he made his money.

He always called his wife Mrs Gilligan as if they were strangers. He'd say, 'Well now, Mrs Gilligan …'

The Gilligans wanted their children to 'have a bit of class'. That's why they sent Ann to the boarding school. They wanted Ann to be 'a lady', a nice, well-brought-up young lady. That's what our school was supposed to do to people.

Ann talked with a very soft, flat accent, the way people from Mullingar do. She was fat and had curly hair. Her mother wanted tall blonde children. The Gilligan children were all fat, and freckly, and curly-haired. Her mother wouldn't give her sweets or cakes. She'd met a woman at the Irish Countrywomen's Association Annual General Meeting in Dublin who'd told her the best thing for making your fat, curly children look like sleek ones, was to give them carrot juice and cabbage juice and never give them any cakes.

Ann was tormented by the other girls saying, 'Ah now, beef to the heels like a Mullingar heifer.' The heifers in Mullingar are supposed to be some of the plumpest in the country.

I bought Ann cakes. I asked my stepmother to send me my post office savings, which had been accumulating towards a record player. I watched her as she sat on my bed in the dormitory and ate through the sweets and cakes, methodically, inexorably. I'd panic in the night wondering where I'd get more money for more sweets and cakes.

I planned to run away from school with Ann. The two of us with our overcoats on over our nightdresses would hitch-hike up the Dublin road at two o'clock in the morning, tell the man we were maids up at the convent, and the nuns had given us such a brutal time that we'd run away. He'd give us a fiver and we'd take the Liverpool boat and get jobs in England.

Ann said I had lovely legs. She looked up from a *Woman's Own* with a half-finished cream slice in her hand. She was reading out a diet: 'Discover the new slim you'. She said, 'You're lucky, you've got lovely legs.' I felt luckier than luck itself.

I looked at my legs as soon as she'd gone. I looked at the other girls' legs. Were mine nicer? Were theirs nicer? Whose were the nicest legs? Ann said, 'Valerie has the nicest legs of all of us.' I prayed Valerie would have an accident with her nice legs.

I said Ann had lovely hair. I used to set her hair: twenty-five curlers and twenty-five hairpins and twenty clips. Ann had a hairdryer so's she could make her curly hair look sleek. Her mother would allow her things like that, but not sweets or cakes. Anything, darling, as long as it made her look sleeker.

We used to spend hours trying to make our hair look sleek.

I stole two eggs from the kitchen. The magazine said, 'You should feed your hair just like you feed your stomach.' They showed a picture of a girl cracking an egg over her head. We cracked eggs on our heads, on our hair. The magazine didn't say what to do next. Mine went like scrambled eggs because I ran the hot tap on it and the water was nearly boiling and I burnt my scalp and had a big mess of sticky egg on it.

We pierced our ears. One of the magazines said if you rubbed some pure alcohol on the lobe of the ear and then quickly jabbed with a very sharp, sterilized needle, having placed a clean cork behind the lobe to be pierced, it would not be painful.

The only alcohol we could think of in the school was the altar wine that was to be turned into the blood of Jesus Christ during Mass, so we thought it must be 'pure alcohol'. The altar boy brought us a cupful for five shillings. Ann crept into my cubicle after lights out. We had a torch. I'd laid out the needle, the cork and the altar wine and a piece of cotton wool on my bedside locker. It looked quite professional. I'd run the needle under the hot tap during evening break.

I was to be done first. Ann said that would be the best. I held the torch in one hand and a little circular mirror that magnified your face in the other.

Ann dipped the cotton wool in the wine. She rubbed it on my right ear lobe. I felt some of the wine dribbling down my neck, cold like a little worm. Ann pushed the cork behind my ear and fixed the ear lobe over it. Then she said, 'Right?' and jabbed with the needle. Ahh! I stiffened all over; I thought she'd driven the needle into my eardrum.

'Shh', she whispered, 'shh,' – slightly petulant. She was the occupied surgeon. Then jab, again. Then jab, jab, jab. My scalp was lifting off, the torch shaking, my eyes burning with tears.

'There,' said Ann finally, leaning back, turning the mirror. 'Look!' I looked and the needle was sticking right through and then into the cork; my ear was an impaled animal, helpless.

'We'll have to turn the needle round a few times,' Ann hissed, 'to make the hole bigger.' She turned it. It was like the dentist tapping a tune on a raw tooth.

She did the second one. Then we put in golden safety pins as we had no earrings. You had to do that to keep the holes open. I took three aspirin. I said to Ann she'd have to wait for hers till tomorrow. I lay on my back, my ears gripping together: one ear, one feeling of pain.

The next day I kept my hair down over my ears and screamed out loud when I caught the comb in one of the pins when I was combing my hair. We got one of the day-girls to buy a pair of earrings for two shillings. We got Valerie to do Ann's ears for her. I couldn't do it.

Then we tried to make our bosoms bigger. We saw an ad for this suction tube thing a woman was holding over one of them to make it bigger. You saw a picture of her: *Before* and *After*. *After* she had a big bosom, like two mountains. Ann said perhaps the suction plunger for clearing the sink would do the trick.

I knelt over Ann, wielding the plunger. After a bit of fiddling about we finally got it to grip the right breast. But then, panic. We couldn't get it off. I was frantically pulling, Ann was screaming and her chest was pulled up like a chicken's when it's being plucked and Doreen, this girl from the North of Ireland, came in and said, 'Ye pair of bloody eejits, have ye no sinse at all?' She rubbed soap round the edge of the plunger and it slipped off. Ann was left with a big red mark round her breast for days—like a target board.

We went on diets together. We set up rigorous schedules for face-cleansing, muscle-toning, hair-conditioning. They'd last less than a week. We went on fruit-eating binges. We went on programmes of squeezing every blackhead in sight and then went on programmes of diligently avoiding even touching them.

We went on walks together. We marched down through the school woods, our coats buttoned against the March winds, chanting Hamlet at the top of our voices. We knew the whole of the 'Ode to the West Wind' by heart, and great chunks of *Paradise Lost*. We gabbled out precis of Irish poems that we'd carefully memorized from our Irish readers. We reeled off Dates of Importance in Irish History, carefully memorized from our history readers. We shouted Caesar's wars to the wind.

We played at being in love together. We pretended Ann was going on a long journey. She was my husband. She was going to Russia. As a spy. We were hugging each other. Kissing each other. Saying, 'My dearest, my darling, I love you, I love you, I always, always will …'

We pretended we were in a film. Ann was the shy, little, poor girl and I was a Man of the World. I was Gregory Peck. I'd take her for a walk, pointing out the trees and flowers. She'd be surprised, awestruck; such knowledge, such sophistication. She'd be humble, prostrate. I'd sweep her in my arms and hold her tightly. I'd protect her from the nasty, horrid world. I'd make her mine.

We gave each other holy pictures for our missals: 'To Dearest Liz, In Rem. of our becoming BFs, God Bless You, Ann.' BFs meant Best Friends. Everyone had a BF. Everyone's missal had holy pictures from different BFs at different times.

One night I wrote Ann a poem. It was about mountains and rivers and rushing waters and her eyes and her hair. It was about her 'silken tresses balanced atop those luminous orbs of wisdom, thine eyes.' It was beautiful, I thought. My heart. Ann's desire.

Valerie found the poem. She read it out to three girls. I could hear them from my cubicle. They were laughing like hyenas. Ha, ha, ha.

I ran out of my cubicle and down the dormitory and one of them saw me and said, 'Oh Jesus, there's Elizabeth, she must have heard us.' I ran on and down to the hockey field and cried till my eyes felt like holes in the wind and my head was the size of the sky.

Ann laughing with Valerie at the poem. My love. I could hear their laughs creaking.

I took the holy pictures and the letters Ann had written to me. I took a rag doll she'd given me for putting my nightdress in, and a handkerchief with 'L' embroidered crookedly in the corner. I put them all in a cardboard box with 'Heinz meanz Beanz' printed on each side. I left them outside her cubicle door with a note saying, 'I never want to talk to you again, Elizabeth.'

I went back into my own cubicle. I got into bed and pulled the sheets over my head. The lights went out. I was lying on my back. I ran my hands up and down my body, under my nightdress.

I felt my nipples, stiffening and standing. I ran my tongue over my lips. I was thinking: one day I'll have a man and he'll be doing this to me; my man will be doing this to me every night and my body will be all white and fiery and he'll be stroking and petting; I never thought of what I'd be doing to him. But I could feel what my own body would be like, so running, so smooth.

I thought: Ann. Ann and her friends. Her BFs. They can all go to hell for all I care. Soon I'll have a man and I'll be with him and he'll be protecting me from their eyes and their laughs.

I didn't know then about the grappling, the bargaining, the closed eyes, the thrusting, the after-sleep, the mouth open and the snores, your own eyes black in the night's blackness, drowning.

∽ 9 ∽

'Women,' said the man from the Department of Education, 'form a vital part of the Civil Service. They hold down jobs in every rung and sector.'

I had visions of hundreds of grey-bunned, twin-setted and pearled spinsters clinging desperately to a swaying ladder. The man from the Department of Education was not there to stimulate our imaginations, however; he had come as part of the Mistress of Studies' Career Guidance Programme.

The Mistress of Studies had gone to one of the English convents for her Easter holidays. (Because the nuns weren't allowed outside the convents, in the sense of staying with relatives, or visiting hotels, they had to holiday in other convents. 'Jaysus,' we'd say, 'The Poor Things.') But the Mistress of Studies had discovered that the English nuns had a fully fledged Career Guidance Programme going for their girls. (They even had some talks on Marriage and Family Planning. But that wasn't to be for the Irish girls.) She came back from her holidays having had her very first swim in a swimming pool, and determined that St Margaret's Boarding School for Young Ladies would have a Career Guidance Programme. Our year was the first year to benefit from such twentieth-century thinking.

The man from the Department of Education made an inauspicious start. He wore a dark grey suit that was far too long in the crotch. He had horn-rimmed glasses that he kept pushing up his nose—a nervous tick. He was like someone who'd spent a long time in a dark room and only crept out occasionally.

He intoned the salary scales and increments women could

get in the Department of Education. His face almost warmed as he moved up the year-by-year increases. We, I seem to remember, remained unmoved.

He had tea with the teachers in the school refectory and folded his thin-sliced bread back on itself and dipped it in his tea. We looked on, horrified, fascinated at his vulgarity. He took out a packet of Woodbines and lit one up—'Hope you don't mind, Sister?' to the nun—and blew smoke everywhere. He went off then in his battered Fiat leaving six neat piles of leaflets about all the things women could do in the Irish Civil Service. The leaflets went yellow and dusty in the Assembly Hall bookstand.

It was our last term at school.

We had our Leaving Certificate examinations to take at the end, 10 June. We knew the sun would shine as it always did during exam times. We would feel very important. Surprised at how quickly we'd become the serious seniors we'd gawped at only such a short time ago. The juniors would be extra nice to us, offering to do all sorts of favours. The teachers would be solicitous: 'How did you do? What was the Lit paper like? Which question did you answer first?' and so on. The nuns would whisper, 'I'm saying a special novena to St Joseph for you dear,' and would let us sleep in on Sunday morning.

We'd have our supper separately from the rest of the school in a room off the kitchen. The 'leavers' ate there every year. It was a privilege. It was supposed to help us relax before the following day's ordeal. We scraped each other's nerves and rattled each other's confidence and barked, like gladiators. 'God I can't remember a thing … Ooh I wish I'd worked harder at Irish … Ah no, really, I'm sure you'll do very well … really …'

After the exams everything for me was a blank. I'd got over loving Ann Gilligan. I could even talk to her without blushing. I'd become Valerie's friend. We went round together being very brittle and cutting.

I thought I might be a very brainy Hayley Mills. I'd pretend I was in a film and flick my hair walking down the corridor and ridge my forehead to show I wasn't just a Pretty Face. Valerie said we should go to Dublin when we left and get a flat and invite fellas in for drinks and things. We said that was the thing.

I got a letter from Jack Hickey. I thought it was a slightly stupid letter, awkward. I didn't say that to anyone. Valerie said, 'He sounds gorgeous. Protestants are terrible rude you know' and gave me an elbow in the ribs and we laughed and all I could see was Jack Hickey in his cricket whites.

I didn't write back immediately. Valerie said, 'You mustn't make a fool of yourself, throwing yourself at him. Keep him guessing.' So, I thought: Let him wait, let's see if he's really in love, let's see if he writes again.

He didn't write again. After six weeks I didn't know what the next step was so I didn't write either. I was the one guessing.

Then we had our career guidance talks.

The Mistress of Studies had fixed Saturday afternoons as the most appropriate time for us to peruse our future careers. The Saturday afternoon following the visit from the man from the Department of Education, a man came who'd been cured at Lourdes. Nobody seemed quite sure what kind of career he might advise us to adopt (other than a general increase in holiness, etc.), but the Mistress of Studies had been given his name by one of the nuns in Dublin when she'd written asking for speakers for her Career Guidance Programme. So he was invited.

The man was rather fat and red-faced. He'd been dying of TB, tuberculosis. He stood on the podium, refusing the comfort of a chair; he was that holy. He occasionally sipped from a carafe of water that the nuns had provided. The carafe of water had been taken from one of the parlours and it was placed on a square table that had a crimson plush tablecloth down to the ground. The table had a matching chair that also stood on the wooden podium.

The man described how the doctors had given up all hope, and how he had only a few months to live and how his sister, who was a most holy woman (a spinster, who'd given up her life to look after her ageing parents and now her dying brother), had secretly saved up for a ticket to Lourdes for the two of them. How she arranged it all and then told him.

He told us how he woke up from his drugged state on the aeroplane and he thought he was winging his way to heaven and that the Aer Lingus air hostess was an angel. The nun was smiling, and nodding, and smoothing her habit down with her hands.

The man said, 'When you are first wheeled out into the main square at Lourdes you feel quite self-conscious but soon you relax as there are hundreds of other people in wheelchairs, on stretchers, on crutches.

'Then,' he said, 'my turn came to go into the baths.' I'd thought that the sick people were wheeled under a mountain spring, where Bernadette the little peasant girl had seen a vision of the Virgin Mary, and fresh mountain water ran over you and your wounds and then you jumped up and threw away your crutches shouting 'Hallelujah' and your crutches wobbled on top of a huge pile of other crutches and wheelchairs and stretchers that people had discarded after a touch of the miracle water.

But no. The man said the baths were quite old, scabrous sort of baths. You didn't even get clean water, you were just slipped in after hundreds of other pilgrims with all their diseases. He said, 'That's a miracle in itself, the way nobody gets a disease from that water.' (You thought: That'll be something to tell the Hickeys, next time they laugh about Lourdes.)

He said, 'The water was freezing. I thought my last hour had come, that my poor diseased, battered body would never stand the shock of the cold, old, water. I clung to my sister's hand.'

Two weeks later the doctors in the Lourdes hospital confirmed that he was cured. There was no sign of TB on his X-ray. He said he still didn't have a certificate because it took a whole team of brilliant doctors months and months of investigation before they proclaimed a Miracle. It was very difficult to get them to agree that a Real Miracle had taken place. Very difficult. Lourdes wasn't all holy water and leaping cripples. Oh no. A very serious, difficult business.

I wished somebody I knew would get terribly sick so's I could take them to Lourdes.

After the man with TB, we had a visit from an 'Old Girl'. Old

Girls were past pupils of the school. There was a special section about them in the School Annual, the Old Girls' section: who was having a baby, and who'd got married, and who'd won an award for this or that. Mostly about babies and marriages though.

This Old Girl was called Oonagh. She'd been working for the United Nations for three years.

She said she got paid ninety dollars a week and we all gasped. She was a secretary to some big shot in the U.N. Secretariat. She told us about having to go out to dinner a lot with visiting dignitaries to New York's poshest restaurants.

She said, 'The United Nations is the most important institution in the history of mankind for keeping the peace. Without it there would be another World War. Nobody wants another World War do they?' she shouted rhetorically from the platform, her dyed New York blonde hair stiff round her pinky-white face.

We said, 'Oh no,' in great and solemn unison. But really I think we would have quite liked one. Grown-ups were always saying, 'Oh that was before the War,' or, 'Well that was during the War, wasn't it?' Or the really old ones would say, 'Now which war do you mean?' They'd turn to you, very patronizing, and say, 'But of course *you* wouldn't remember that.' They were very proud of their damned wars as far as we could see.

Anyway it was just around the time of the trouble in the Congo and this Oonagh girl told us that the United Nations was keeping the peace there. We knew some Irish soldiers had gone out and we were told that a few of them had been eaten. We all called each other 'Big Ballubas' that term, as an insult. We didn't argue with the girl about the peace because we only got the papers once a week and nobody in school ever discussed politics.

So we listened to Oonagh very respectfully, and felt sorry for her. You could tell she was going to be a spinster with her soft mohair top and expensive silk scarf. We weren't fooled by all the talk of dinners, and ninety dollars a week, and wars.

Then we had a woman and a man from a theatre troupe. We liked them. The nuns got very agitated. The Mistress of Studies had thought they were opera singers from the Gaiety Theatre but they just sang sparkly songs from the twenties and said, 'Darlings, life in the theatre is hell, but it gets into your blood —like a drug.'

The woman had masses of powder on, and very red lipstick. Her hair was dyed black and she smoked king-size cigarettes in this long black holder non-stop. She was called Maureen and the man was called Brendan. Maureen did most of the talking and Brendan smiled at her and burst out laughing and pointed his finger at her and covered his mouth with his hands and his two eyebrows went up in a point into his forehead.

Maureen told us she peed on the stage her first night in her first public pantomime; she was a fairy. She said she nearly died of shame. She wore masses of rings. She did a quick rendition of Lady Macbeth trying to rub the blood off her hands after she'd murdered the king, because we were doing Macbeth for our exams. The rings clicked as she rubbed her hands: 'What, what, will these little hands ne'er come clean …' She looked tormented. Then she recited Padraic Pearse's poem: 'I do not grudge them, Lord I do not grudge …' Pearse had written the poem for his mother the night before the British executed him. The nuns thought that was beautifully done.

Then we had a woman who ran a secretarial college in Dublin. It was called Miss Lavelle's Finishing School. The name was painted up in gold lettering over the door. (Inside, though, there was nothing but desks that had grime and sweat from hundreds of elbows and hands and fingers and old grey typewriters that had to be crashed at to get up any speed or make a carbon copy. That you learnt about much—years—later.)

Miss Lavelle said, 'Every young lady now needs to have some skill she can fall back on if times get hard.' Times getting hard meant being widowed—suddenly, tragically, poetically. Left with three young children to feed and clothe.

Miss Lavelle said her girls did very well for themselves. She said they had good jobs in the Civil Service and one of them was a personal secretary to a bank manager. One had even started up a little business of her own.

Besides typing and shorthand, Miss Lavelle said she also taught elocution, English Literature, simple mathematics and deportment. She said she was sure that Young Ladies like ourselves, with the lovely education the holy nuns had given us and all, wouldn't need such things.

We sat through each visit, sometimes amused, sometimes amazed, sometimes plain bored. We never felt involved. These were visitors from another world. We thought: Soon we're going to leave school. We'll be free, free to do anything. Free to stay in bed all day. Free to drink coffee till four in the morning. Free to wear what we like.

We thought: We have no intention of signing up with some lower-class little secretarial school. No, not on your life. Jobs—ha! We were going to be free for a bit and then we were going to be married. (Apart from Geraldine Doyle who was potty anyway.) We were all going to have smart husbands who would have smart jobs and lots of money. We were going to have tiny button-nosed children in perpetually clean dresses. This was our pre-destined destiny. Secretaries, United Nations, Big Shots—ha!

Some girls would go to University. Perhaps three or four every year. This was because ours was a posh school and there was a tradition of a few professional career girls and blue stockings emerging annually. That was what the tradition was.

But soon there would be the Last Day of Term. We would all cry and think we were terribly old and feel a bit frightened. We would give our cubicles to our friends in the year below us, and pictures of Marilyn Monroe and Russ Conway to the juniors. Our parents would come in their cars and pick us up. We would be strained and pale after our long two weeks of exams. We would hug each other and shake hands with the nuns and accept their kisses on our cheeks. The school would sing 'Auld Lang Syne', and we would cry and the other girls would cry and even some of the nuns would shed a tear into their big white handkerchiefs with numbers in the corners.

Our parents would take us home. On the way many of us would stop for roast beef dinners in hotels. A celebration.

∽ ∽

PART TWO

'France!' said the woman on the bus coming in from the airport. 'Merciful Jesus, I was there once meself. I've never known a people with worse smelling breath than that lot. And the food they'd give ya! It wouldn't be worth feedin' to the dogs. Me husband and I had to stay three days there in Paris once. I thought we'd never get out of it—ugh!'

I smiled what I hoped was a supremely condescending smile. The woman didn't even seem to notice. She just went on and on like that. Everything reduced to an irritation. You could hear her—Rome, Athens, Africa: Merciful Jesus! The sweat, the heat, the noise, the smell. Something. She began to irritate me. I hadn't liked France that much either. But I'd never thought of saying so.

We'd left school. Before Valerie could come to Dublin, the local doctor had cast an eye on her; she gave him encouragement and in horror and haste her mother sent her off to Italy. She taught English to the children of a Count, slept with Italian writers and Hungarian refugees. She also learnt how to de-hair her legs with beeswax.

I sat at home. I got my exam results. They were neither brilliant nor disastrous.

Whenever my father noticed I was around he would say, 'We must get you into the history faculty, Liz,' and then go back to his study. He was writing an exhaustive history of the time of the Fir Bolg in Ireland.

I went into town and met school friends for coffee and we talked about boys and our bodies and clothes. I read books, intermittently and haphazardly. I made myself things to wear. Days passed by. Pleasantly or unpleasantly? I can't really remember. Nobody had ever said things like, 'Things only happen if you make them happen.' So I suppose I was just waiting for something to happen to me.

At school our plan had been to be free. Free of our parents, free of petty restrictions. We hadn't thought: To be free you have to have money, to have money you had to have a job. The nuns hadn't told us that. I could chant Caesar's battles; I could recite the 'Ode to the West Wind' without pause. That was all.

This Saturday afternoon in October a friend of my step-mother's came to the house. She considered herself to be the Jolly type, going round her friends' houses giving them loud, healthy advice on dropped wombs and apple jelly.

She settled herself into one of the armchairs with a cup of tea and a cigarette. You could always tell she'd been there by the cig-arette butts ringed with lipstick she left crushed in the ashtray. Mary was on the edge of her chair. Anxious to appear jolly and healthy enough.

'So, what is our Eliza doing these days?' She looked at me, then Mary. I hated being called Eliza. For a minute I felt like pushing her damned stupid hat down over her eyes.

I said, 'Oh nothing much.'

'And plans for the future?' she asked, beady. *You must have plans for the future. Everyone has. Tomorrow for instance. Come along then. Brace up.* That's the sort of look she'd give you.

I said, 'I'm going to the University.' Usually that kept them quiet for a bit. 'Very nice dear,' they'd say and almost pat you on the head. This one said, 'But Elizabeth darling, enrolments were closed a week ago.'

Panic. Clear your throat. 'Ehm … well my father said …'

'But I'm afraid your father is wrong, dear.' (Dare you contra-dict him you silly old bag? But she was winning. Mary was al-most falling off her chair in a concentration of concern.)

'I know, Mary,' said this awful woman. 'Why not send her to France for six months? I've sent three of my girls there and they've all had a very good time. I know just the family who would take her on as an au pair.' And so they arranged it. They might have been discussing the difficulties of bringing up pedi-gree dogs—this kennel, or that, now which do you think?

Four weeks later I was heading for Paris in a camel-hair coat, clutching a barn brack (a present for Madame and Monsieur). Coming down the steps off the aeroplane I chucked the brack over the side. A little, dark, French mechanic caught up with me just at the customs gate, the battered cake in his oily hands: 'C'est a vous Mademoiselle?'—all smiles and delighted with himself. I stuffed it in the bin in the ladies' lav.

Paris, I thought, was the most awful place in the world. After two weeks I made friends with another Irish girl, also an au pair. We used to meet in the Avenue Royale and fill ourselves up with French bread, sandwiches and water—the coffee was too expensive. Anyway, this girl said, it makes you sterile, barren.

At the beginning I remember just being hungry most of the time. Madame ate very little because of her figure and Monsieur ate lunch at a café near his work and just snacked on salami or cheese in the evening. I used to pray for the children to not finish their food, and then gobble it while Madame wasn't looking.

At night I'd lie awake and think of roast beef and gravy and potatoes and two veg, and compose letters of my tortures to my father. I never actually wrote them.

The Dumonts, the couple for whom I worked, were a young middle-class couple with two children, a flat in Montparnasse, and a fixed income. M. Dumont was a dentist. He left the flat at 7.00 a.m. and returned at 7.30 p.m. Madame was a housewife. She kept their flat chic and *bijou* like their friends' flats, and amused her lovers.

While I took the baby Dumont, Pierre, for what were supposed to be long walks in the park, but were in fact trips to the cafés in the Avenue Royale, and while M. Dumont was being *un bon dentiste,* Madame Dumont was rolling round her marital bed with one of her lovers. Alternatively they rolled on the living room floor on a blonde rug, which her husband had brought her from somewhere exotic.

I came home early from our walk one day. Baby Pierre had a bloody nose, having careered, pushchair and all, into a lamppost. There were Madame and her current lover on the floor; there was I with Pierre bawling in his pushchair. I stood looking foolishly down at them, and they looked up at me: Madame straight, the lover over his shoulder. Then Madame made a marvellous

French 'pprT sound and they gathered their bodies up like puppets and took them into the bedroom.

I was horrified. Fascinated. Amazed.

Madame became very sweet to me. She stopped shouting at
me in great torrents of French. She couldn't do enough for Lee-
tle Irish. She gave me her clothes that she was bored with, silk
scarves and beautifully tailored tweed skirts. She said I must have
my hair bobbed so I would look like a French mam'selle. My
ears felt naked and cold afterwards. She said, I looked almost chic.
'Presque.'

Madame always looked chic. It was an art, she said, a timeless
art of French women. I had never met anyone so totally materi-
alistic; she was sophisticated sin incarnate. I tried to copy her.

Monsieur was very gentle towards her, particularly when they
had friends in. They would dress up, Madame like a radiant pea-
cock; they would touch each other's hands across the table, and
click their eyes together. Their friends, who also had lovers, said
the Dumonts were a beautiful couple, so in love.

Madame never imparted any other knowledge or experience
of l'amour to me. I was too shy to ask. Was it age difference, or just
jealousy? That glint in a woman's eye when men are around—
like with my boy.

The boy was blonde. He was the same height as me and had
green eyes. It was the combination of blonde and green that
made you look at him. He looked back with those quite unblinking green eyes.

We started having coffees together. My evening off we had
more coffees together. He said his father was a film director; he
made underground films. (Underground? Underground where?
How? He laughed at you then till his green eyes went into hard
slits like a cat's.) He said he was a writer: he wrote poems and was
also writing a novel. A novel about the philosophy of humanism
and the atomic bomb.

He wrote you a poem. Your French wasn't quite good
enough. You took it home to the flat. You and M. Dumont carefully translated it. A vicarious pleasure—such a thing to say to a
little girl! Madame gave you a funny look. Monsieur said, 'You

must meet some of our younger friends. We will have a party.'

You thought: Things are definitely looking up; I have a boyfriend and now we're going to have a party.

The blonde boy and Helen, an Irish girl, came to the party. The blonde boy was called Henri. He wore blue jeans and a black polo-neck sweater. He had a habit of holding his head on one side when he was listening to someone.

He was listening to Madame Dumont. You could see the light and shade on the bones of her back; her smooth, brown, French back. Her little black dress with its deep V showed off her back so nicely—the light and shade on it.

What was she saying? He was laughing. He laughed so seldomly. Talked so little. A real listener. You'd thought it was just to you. Madame was gesticulating. Now he was saying something. Madame was laughing. She touched his cheek lightly with her hand, gently, protectively.

Monsieur was talking to a slim girl with long hair, like a madonna. I felt frantic. Everyone cheating everyone else. Smiling, glinting, touching each other up, preparing ... it's horrible. A teacher from the Sorbonne, where I went to improve my awful schoolgirl French, was saying something about Victor Hugo and bath plugs and on and on and on.

Madame came over to her husband—*must keep an eye on him, a little bit for you, a little bit for me, and then we're happy, quits, right?*

She was leading Henri by the hand. 'But your friend is so charming, Elizabeth,' she said to me, looking at him. Too charming. You longed for the roof of the sky to fall in and the whole circus to be over. No more talking, no more laughing, no more knives.

Henri found you outside the door sitting on the stairway. He lit you both up cigarettes, and you sipped brandy from his glass. You were bright. He said, 'Oh but that Madame of yours is a coquette.' You were brighter. You could see his eyes, liquid, in the darkness.

Music was coming from the room now. He said, 'Where is your bedroom?' You told him. He got up and took your hand.

'Let's go.' You were surprised, but you went. You were terrified Madame would come in and find you: 'Qu'est-ce qui passe …?' You were on the bed, your mouths sucking each other. He was kissing you all over and his hands were pushing your breasts and one minute he got a bit rough because you seemed to pull away. He was quite quick.

Afterwards you lay very quietly. You looked at his blonde head on your shoulder.

After a bit you said, 'Does that mean I'm not a virgin any more?' He jumped up and said, 'What? What?'—frightened-sounding, and angry. 'What do you mean? What is this you are saying?' He reached out for a cigarette and you had one too and you wanted him to lie down again. You told him then about Valerie and how she had shown you how to break the seal on 'our honeypots', as she said. It was so you wouldn't be embarrassed by it later. He laughed then and he looked like a little boy with his fair hair and his clear eyes and together you finished his brandy and he said, 'Now you must sleep.'

When I woke up he was gone. The bed was crumpled. A sad bed. A used bed. I made it up. That was the last time I saw him. Afterwards he had made love with Madame, and what's more, she told me.

Paris became doubly lonely after that. A big draughty city. Everyone shouting. I spent two precious francs on a guide to the Louvre. I didn't get further than the hallway. I thought, If I had a dog even, let alone a man, a boyfriend, just something to come round with me, then it wouldn't be so bad. I walked with Pierre in his pushcart from the flat, to the park, to the café, and back. I thought, at least people can't laugh at me; I look as if I'm doing something.

Helen and I went a few times to these 'multinational dis-cotheques'. All the boys seemed to assume that all au pairs were whores; we assumed they were all sex maniacs. They were strained evenings, sitting in the discotheques with the multina-tionals, burping over Coca-Cola. One came home feeling dis-satisfied and exhausted.

I tried to feel guilty. 'I've committed a mortal sin,' I'd say to myself. 'If I die I'll go to hell for ever, and ever.' I went along to Notre Dame in my soberest clothes. I knelt in the most uncomfortable place I could find. I went to confession. I had to shout out my sin because the priest was old and deaf and my French wasn't so good. My voice must have ricocheted round the domed walls: *'J'ai avais faire l'amour avec un mauvais garçon.'* The priest kept saying, 'Comment?' in this wheezy, cranky voice. Finally, he said to say three Hail Marys and be more careful in future. I never knew whether he understood or not. Would I go to another priest? Helen said, 'Stop being such a guilty Catholic.'

I didn't realize I had stopped being a Catholic until a woman with painted red nails and black hair asked me if I was a 'proper' Catholic still. This was at one of the Dumonts' parties. In France, she said, everyone was a Catholic in name but none of them went to church or believed in sins or any of that. I said, 'Yes,' then, 'No,' then said, 'Well no, I suppose I'm not really.' The lady shrieked with laughter and went off to tell about the Irish girl who couldn't make up her mind whether she was a Catholic or not.

I got up very early one Sunday and took Pierre and the other child to Mass. The whole church seemed vast and cold, with the priest and a few old people attending—tiny, dusty figures acting out a forgotten ritual. I went home feeling reduced, smaller somehow. Something that had taken up so much time and emotion had gone quite dead.

I wrote a letter to a priest at home. I said, 'I've lost The Faith.' He wrote back a long and impassioned letter about the pagan French, how sophistication was an evil thing, and that I was to come home soon to Ireland and bathe my soul in the pure waters of Irish Catholicism and bask in the faith of my fathers. There were pages of it.

No thunderbolts came from the sky. I didn't even dream about it. I felt slightly embarrassed when, a year later, a spotty and earnest lecturer at the University, a visitor from Oxford, asked me to delineate the theological traumas I had been through upon giving up my religion. He kept on about it, thinking my reply of 'None' was Irish modesty.

A visit from the priest, and a letter from me, happened upon my parents' doorstep the same day. The priest said he thought I should be brought home. I said I wanted to come home. The priest said I was having religious difficulties. I said Madame Dumont had a lover. Mary sent me an air ticket by return of post. Madame followed me round whining for the last week. I never had the nerve to slap her face. I just thought: Keep calm, it will soon be over.

∽ 2 ∽

I came back from Paris able to speak French slightly better than when I left; no longer a virgin, no longer a Catholic.

Mary kept saying, 'Oh dear, it must have been terrible for you.' She was referring to Madame being a loose woman. I said, 'Yes, it was terrible.' My father said, 'Well now, it's nice to have you back.' That was at dinner the first night home. I was a stranger, sitting down eating roast chicken and potatoes and carrots with these two other strangers. They never asked me about Paris or Madame after that. Just a few questions the first night: *Did you go sight-seeing much? What did you do in the evenings? Is butter really fifteen shillings a pound in Paris?* Then we didn't talk about it any more.

A few days later the priest called round. Mary left us alone in the dining room. We sat on the stiff dining chairs; he laid his hands and arms awkwardly on the table like legs of lamb.

'Well now my dear child, tell me about it.' His head was slightly lowered, almost as if he were in the confessional. I felt an urge to splay it all out before him: me, Henri, Madame, her husband, my loneliness, my confusion, and the hurt, because somebody must explain the stupid brutality of that boy, of life.

I said, 'I just don't believe any longer, Father.' The rest I kept to myself. You mustn't frighten people, mustn't upset them. All the priest wanted to know is why you no longer wanted to go to church. You must tell him. Simple things. Rituals.

The priest said, 'Elizabeth—you don't mind if I call you Elizabeth?—we all of us go through great periods of doubt. Even the Pope himself has to wrestle with the Devil.' He said, 'We must be patient. God will return to us. God is testing us.' I'd heard it all before. I kept quiet. *It will be over sooner that way.*

What if you said, 'I loved someone, Father. I wanted to touch him. We touched each other and loved. Everyone needs that, Father. But then he left ... he didn't even say goodbye'? You were beginning to sound like a cliché. The songs, the pop songs that almost made you cry: *I'm just a lonely girl, lonely and blue.*

But I said nothing to the priest. Just 'Yes Father' and 'No Father' and 'Certainly Father'. He said I must come to confession and then receive Holy Communion. I started at that. Communion! And me with a mortal sin. I forgotten I'd given up believing. Even still.

Mary was solicitous. I felt vaguely important—a mortal sinner at eighteen. I went to Mass with her and she watched me through her hands. I cried once during High Mass because the sound of the organ was like someone in pain and I was feeling wobbly because I had my period. I thought, Soon I'll tell them all that I've stopped believing; meantime it's better to be kind and just tag along.

The priest came round every so often with books on saints' lives, and then even some modern books about people who looked after drunks and layabouts and wiped up their sick and never shouted at them. The priest said, 'There are a million ways to serve God.' I thought of Madame saying, 'There are a million ways of making love.' I thought: Millions and millions of ways and how is it I can't see one?

Mary said, 'Something will turn up, not to worry,' and took me round to her friends' houses for coffee. The coffee seemed awful after Paris. Mary said, 'Oh mind out now with your high falutin' ways.' That was the last I said about coffee.

Mary's friends asked politely about France and one of them had once been to the Mediterranean and she showed us colour photos of her holiday. The photos had gone liver-coloured with age.

When they'd asked a few questions about Paris they started talking about their babies, or their insides (did every woman over the age of thirty-five have something wrong with her womb?) and then their husbands. They talked about their husbands' appetites or how difficult it was to get them to change their socks. They never said things like, 'He thinks capitalism a terrible thing,' or, 'He's very excited by the space race to the moon.' The French women used to do that; Madame and her friends would swap their husband's heads. These women swapped their feet, or their indigestion.

Valerie came back from Italy. She rang up one evening. I sat in my coat, cigarette in hand, and her voice was coming down the line, small and funny. She said, 'I've *loads* to tell you.' Then we couldn't think of anything to say so we said we'd meet for lunch the next day. Valerie suggested lunch—it sounded very sophisticated. Before it'd been just for coffees.

We had lunch in this café where all the au pairs that come to Dublin eat. I pitied them for a bit, remembering what it had been like, but as soon as you no longer feel the pain of it yourself you almost think other people are stupid to complain.

Valerie had had her hair dyed blonde in Italy and then gone skiing and the sun had turned it bright orange. She looked like one of those dolls—their hair green, or any sort of colour. She'd put on weight but it suited her; her hips filled up her skirt and they didn't look frumpish or flabby, they just looked like big wide hips. She wore a tan sweater with a scooped neck and a string of beads: plastic, she said, but they looked like amber. She tossed her head. Men looked at her. You could see her laughing right into their faces.

She talked about the men she'd been to bed with. The little one with the habit of pulling his nose, who turned out to be married with five children and a wife in Sicily. The wife had come, flaming with anger, to collect him. The tall aesthetic one who talked about love and politics and played 'The Red Flag' at six in the morning and the concierge came running out into the courtyard, shouting. There was the passionate one who was once taken to hospital stuck stiff to the woman he was making love to because her husband had come in halfway through and she'd clammed up with the shock of it.

I wondered why she left—all those men, why come back to Ireland? She was quick to see I was becoming skeptical. 'Tell me about yourself. What was Gay Paree like then? Go on, tell it all.'

All. I told about Henri. I told about our making love. I didn't tell about his creeping off to Madame's bedroom. I said, I crept off to Monsieur's bedroom. I said Monsieur and I had a passionate affair. I had Monsieur and I leaping at each other like mad beasts whenever Madame's back was turned.

Valerie said, 'Jaysus, I know. Once you get a taste for it you can't stop.' I almost laughed then but choked into the coffee cup, 'Mmm.'

It was a taste for loneliness, but a new kind of taste. Not the loneliness of being home, being ten or twelve or fifteen. That was quiet and formal and stretched, how the sea on a dull day stretches to the horizon, stiff and flat. Not even the loneliness of school, of lying in your bed, of wondering when would life start with all the love and roses and linked arms. No, quite a new taste. Of being taken and held and touched. Of being left. Forbidden tastes—like Eve in the Garden of Eden. A beautiful, beautiful fruit. She tastes it. Aha! Down they come on her. *Out you go my dear, this minute, the wilderness awaits you ...*

Valerie had a job in a boutique just down the road. She said to come down with her and have a look around. The boutique was run by this girl with very straight black hair and clear skin. She wore a long dress, a sort of elongated t-shirt. You could see her hipbones under the dress. Valerie introduced us and the girl gave a quick up-down look. Too tall? Or short? Or fat? Or thin? She had her dresses to sell and the bodies had to fit them. Not, as you might think, the other way around.

This girl must have been only three or four years older than us. Yet, she was hard—her face was a mask, a beautiful, made-up, polished mask, but the mask had also become her face. She said, 'Make us a cup of coffee, Val, before we re-open.' Valerie was in awe of her, you could see that. She lit up a cigarette and then walked over to one of these tree-type hat stands where the clothes were hanging on big red and purple hangers. 'Try this on,' she said to me. She handed me a long red dress, the back criss–cross tied like tennis shoes or a German sausage.

I went into one of these changing cubicles. My head stuck out over the top. My hands were sticky. I was sure I'd mark the dress, ruin it. I came out. The girl came over and stood me in front of a mirror. This way, that way, pulling, fluffing my hair out, smoothing the dress over my behind, tucking it up under my bosoms. Unembarrassed, I could have been a dressmaker's dummy, the way this girl touched me, unashamedly.

She stood back. 'Have you ever tried modelling?'

'No,' I said, giggling. Me, a model?

'You should,' she said. She didn't notice the giggle. 'You've got a good figure; with a bit of training I think you'd make a very good model. Off and on we need someone to model our stuff—we have sort of fashion show happenings in the street to advertise our wares.'

I looked at myself in the mirror. A white face, black hair. Green eyes. 'A real colleen,' one of the teachers at school had said, and had made me Caitlin Ni Houlihan in her history play.

The coffee was ready. I took the dress off. The girl was rear-ranging things in the window. She'd forgotten? Valerie and I drank our coffee. Valerie grinning—she'd introduced me, she was part of it.

I said I must go. The girl said, 'Bye now.' Obviously she'd for-gotten. She was pinning back a jersey dress on a plaster model in the tiny window.

I didn't get home till late that afternoon. My father said he wanted to talk to me in his study. When I was small I used to go and sit in his study. He had a big oaken desk and I used to climb under the arch where your knees were supposed to go and sit there while he worked. I can still hear his pen squeaking across the paper over my head. That was before he remarried. By then I was too big to sit in there anyway.

'Elizabeth, my dear child' he started. It was going to be seri-ous. *Elizabeth, my dear child.* He said, 'Your stepmother and I are worried about you. Spending so much time in your room, or mooning about the house. It's not good, you know, at your age.' One hand was resting on his desk, on top of a manuscript. Mary must have said, 'I think you should talk to Elizabeth.' He'd never have thought of it himself.

I took a cigarette out of my bag and lit it. He looked surprised. He knew so little about me really. I'd been smoking for four weeks, ever since I came back from Paris. He hadn't noticed.

He looked at his desk and then at me. What had Mary said to him? He said, 'I think you should get a job really. Just to get you out of the house a bit. I've been talking to some people at the College.'

So they'd arranged it already. I felt bitter, and then I didn't mind. Why not? Perhaps a job would be better than hanging around here. College? I might meet some people, make friends.

'You should be getting around a bit, making friends, meeting people. You're only young once.' He made eighteen sound like a heart condition. He said, 'We could set off together in the mornings—like proper workers.' That was the bargain then. The two of you.

'What sort of job might I do?' I liked the thought of us setting off together in the mornings in his little grey Fiat.

The people at the College said I could have a job as a filing clerk in the library. My pay would be five pounds, ten shillings a week and I could eat lunch in the college canteen.

The library was run by a woman called Miss Gore-Browne. 'Browne with an E' she'd say whenever she spelled her name for anyone. She wore long tweed skirts and her bosom sagged inside heavy cardigans. Mary said she was 'aristocracy come down in the world'. She had BO and her bedsitter in Sandymount was filled with heavy dark furniture—all she could save from the auction of her family's country seat in Sligo. Miss Gore-Browne knew every book in the library. The students would think up really obscure volumes to ask her about and she'd be striding across the library and picking it out, whistling a *zzz* through her teeth.

I hated the students. It was like a club, their College. They'd smell an outsider by instinct. The students with their easygoing ways and their long hair and their freedom—they'd cut you dead as quick as look at you if you weren't one yourself. Walking across the quadrangle became a torture; I was always waiting to slip on the cobblestones, or for my knickers to fall down, or something. The students would be there, waiting. I sat in the office next door to the library and kept the index up to date and licked envelopes and made tea and sometimes read books that came in.

I only ate in the canteen once. I sat by myself at a table and ate off a tin tray. Irish stew, jelly and cream, coffee and a cake. We'd all gone shuff-shuffling up the line, picking out things from under glass covers, like well-trained animals: pick, pick. Some of the girls just had crackers and cheese and milk, others went overboard and grasped things and pushed their way to the tables to sit down and you could almost see their faces flat into the dish, gobbling.

Girls always seemed to be like that, either picking or stuffing.

I thought the meal would never be over. The canteen was very hot and the students were all shouting at each other across tables and banging their trays down. I felt the weight of my hand lifting the food up and my mouth opening and closing on it. The noise of chewing it and then swallowing it in lumps. I went through every piece. Getting up and walking out was going to be the hardest part. I knocked my bag against this boy's head as I was leaving—'Look out will you,' he said, turning, and I ran up the stairs and out of the College and down to the river and thought, I'll never go back there, never.

After that I went down to the river every lunchtime. I'd lean over the parapet and always expect to see something horrible floating just below the surface. The river was like a murderer.

I thought I was very tragic. I thought if somebody tall and handsome and brave came up to me I'd tell him how sad I was. I'd tell them about Jack Hickey and about Henri, the blonde boy. I'd be mysterious. I'd say, 'It all began with my father you know...'

I'd go for walks and look at men and women together. I'd think some of those women were so damn ugly, and how did they do it? All of them with men linking their arms.

A boyfriend. Somebody to go to the pictures with. Somebody to walk through College with and show those students. Somebody to say you're this or you're that. Somebody to hold you.

How to go about it? Stand on the Metal Bridge with a sign round your neck: *Please I need a friend*? Pass a note to one of the students saying that you'd sleep with him? How do you get a boyfriend?

❧ 3 ❧

My father's study at the College looked out on the old Irish houses of Parliament and down a wide street with four lanes of traffic and tall buildings on either side. Sometimes the buildings could be friendly, showing you their gothic tops or ornate, balconied attics. Other times they would threaten to crush you down flat.

I used to sit in the study if I was early back from my lunch hour walk. If he was there we'd make coffee with the electric kettle Mary had given him, he'd read *The Irish Times* and I might just look out the window, or read a magazine that I'd bought at the bookstand across the road.

It was a Friday. I'd got paid before lunch. The brown envelope was in my coat pocket. I'd bought one pound's worth of magazines. Mary would say I was crazy. I would say, 'What's the point of earning money if you can't spend it on the things you like?' She'd say, 'Some people have no consideration.'

I was looking at this magazine. There was a photo of a group of American teenagers who'd gone into the Himalayas to pray and meditate with an Indian guru. They were all staring straight out of the picture. You'd think people who were praying and fasting would be very disinterested in their physical appearance, but not these Americans. You could see the strain on the girls' faces and their very washed and brushed hair with maybe a flower pinned at one side. The men held their faces very carefully too, looking out. Mary would say, 'Oh those hippies, they're disgusting.' But it wasn't that. They were so frightened, so strained, just like girls at a party or dance, terrified not to look acceptable.

There was a knock on the door. I said, 'Come in,' and the door swung open and there was a man with thick curly black hair and a red scarf round his neck, carrying a sheaf of files and papers. Not a student? A lecturer?

'Hello,' he said, and swung the door to behind him. 'I'm sorry to disturb you but I've come looking for the Prof who knows all about these Fir Bolg men.'

I said, 'Professor O'Sullivan will be back at 2.30 p.m.' I was sitting at my father's desk. I put my arms over the magazine so this man wouldn't see it.

'His secretary, are you?' he asked.

'No,' I said, 'his daughter.' That should quiet him down, I thought.

'Aha,' and he sat down on the sofa where Father's manuscripts and students' essays were piled up. He started looking through them. I thought: The cheek.

'Instead of sitting in this stuffy little office why not come out for a drink with me while we wait for your father?' he said. 'My name's Colin.' And he gave me a broad smile as if I wouldn't, obviously, refuse. I didn't refuse.

We walked across the quadrangle. I felt sorry for the poor girls on their own.

Colin walked very fast. He linked my arm crossing the road. He was one of those people who made everything a we-together situation very quickly if he liked you.

The pub we went into had these paintings of hunting scenes all round the walls. The paintings were in pastel colours with pale horses, pale horsemen, and a sick-looking fox with a huge tail and huge eyes. The bar stools and chairs were covered in chintz. The bar was full of people, mostly men, shouting at one another, standing less than a foot away from each other's faces and shouting.

I said I'd have a gin and tonic. Colin said, 'Go on, be a devil, have something more exotic.' I said, 'Okay, Benedictine.' It was all I could think of. Mary had been given a bottle for Christmas and kept it in the sideboard.

Colin said he was a television producer. He was working on a series of historical programmes—that's why he wanted to see the Professor, my father. He was The Expert on the Fir Bolg.

He said television work was quite fun but got boring like any other job. I was half listening. I was thinking: I'll become his girl-friend and become famous on television.

'And what do you do, sad eyes?' he said.

I flicked my eyes (were they sad eyes?) and said, 'I'm working in the library—but just as a filler-in.'

'A filler-in for what?' he said.

'Oh,' I said, 'Before taking First Arts next year. I've just come back from Paris, so I can't enrol till September.' An inspiration, that one.

'A proper little blue stocking?' he said and was grinning and I felt myself suddenly a bit colder inside. But then we had three more drinks and he walked me back to the library and I felt like dancing across the quadrangle and the cobblestones were like springs to my feet and anything, anything was possible. At about four o'clock I had five cups of tea and then I went home. I told Miss Gore-Browne I was feeling sick—my first hangover.

We went to the theatre and he kissed me and said I was his favourite lady. A favourite among how many? I thought, but did-n't say anything, and jumped on the thought and buried it. We had dinner after the theatre and he listened and it was almost like God listening: 'Tell me exactly what the problem is, and we'll solve it.'

He drove home and the city was quiet and the roads opened up like long carpets of moonlight for us. We kissed in the car outside the house and I was kissing him and kissing him, and then he pulled back a little and he pinched my nose between his thumb and finger and said, 'It will all come to you soon enough, one day.' I wanted to say 'Take me and keep me and let me live with you and in you and …' On the front steps he gave me a for-mal kiss on the cheek and said, 'We mustn't keep the Professor's daughter out too late, must we?' and then he was jumping down the steps and gone.

I went in and made myself a cup of tea and sat for a while in the kitchen and thought if I were with him, with him all the time I wouldn't have to worry any more about not doing any-thing. I would just be.

One night he came to dinner to talk to Father about the Fir

Bolgs. He'd sketched out a script and Father was checking it. He arrived very sober and in a dark suit with pinstripes—a gangster's suit from Chicago. He had a wide, salmon-pink tie. He called Father 'Sir'.

I'd spent the whole day changing the furniture round in the house. I was pinning up an Aubrey Beardsley poster in the hallway and Mary said, 'Take that down at once,' and I burst into tears and said she was an old witch.

The zip got stuck in my favourite dress and I got red in the face and got a whiff of sweat smell from under my arm and rushed back into the bathroom and lashed talc under my arms and cursed Mary for not allowing me to have deodorant. She said it gave people cancer.

I put on some eye make-up. Some brown stick and some mascara. Some of Mary's powder on my nose and chin. Some scent —a drop behind each knee, a drop behind each ear, a drop between the breasts. Those, said the magazine, are the erogenous zones—the places for perfume.

During dinner I said, the words bumping out, 'One of the distinctive physical characteristics of the Fir Bolg was their Mediterranean features. Dark, flashing eyes.' Father looked over and said, 'Well now, I didn't know you knew anything about the Fir Bolg, Lizzie.' I blushed hot, even in my eyes, and said, 'Oh, a teacher told us that at school.' I'd read it that afternoon in one of Father's books.

When he was going I stood between my parents at the door. Colin shook hands with each of us. I wanted to run down the path after him, hug him. He turned and gave a wave at the gate.

'Interesting young man,' my father said. I looked at him. It was the first time I thought his judgement imperfect.

∞ **4** ∞

I was waiting for the phone to ring. I kept picking it up to listen to the purring sound to make sure it was working. I rang the operator. In a crackly voice—could he ring me as I thought maybe our phone was out of order? I put the phone down. It rang.

'Operator here, Miss, your phone seems bang on.' I put the phone down. Got up and lit a cigarette. Mary came through the hall. 'Aren't you getting cold sitting there?' A pause, then, 'Try not to smoke so many cigarettes, Elizabeth, it makes you look so old.' Old is it? I thought, I'm as old as the caves in Kerry. I'm as old as pain.

The phone rang. I ran and picked it up, heart beating, thudding. It was the operator. 'Suppose you wouldn't like to come out for a pint some night, darling?' he said, his voice honeyed. 'Oh God,' I said and slammed down the phone.

Why doesn't he ring? Oh why, why, why?

Why don't I ring him? What would I say? 'Hello Colin, it's me, Lizzie, you remember me? How are things? I just thought I'd ring you and see how you were, you know.'

You know. I couldn't ring him. Why? You just can't. Girls wait to be rung. Unless they're whores or something. Those are the rules. If he wanted to see you he'd ring. If he didn't, he didn't. Maybe he was sick. Lying alone in his flat, quietly dying. I didn't even know where he lived. Maybe a stench was coming from under his doorway. Milk bottles and papers piled outside. Maybe he'd be found, bloated and green, like that dead seal we once found washed up by the sea.

I'd just ring him and see if he was all right. I didn't know his number. I'd get it from the switchboard girl at the television station.

I got the number. I said I was a concerned friend, just back from Paris. The girl said, 'We're not supposed to, you know.' I said, 'I know, but it is rather urgent.'

I rang. His voice answered. He didn't sound dying. He sounded fine. I listened to him for a bit saying, 'Hello, Hello,' then more angrily, 'Look, who is this?' Then I put the phone down.

I went up to the bathroom. My hands were trembling. My mouth tasted awful with the cigarettes. I looked at myself in the mirror. I made faces—faces like we used to make at school.

'You're horrible, horrible, I hate you, you're a fool, a flea-bitten eejit …'

I watched the tears popping out and coming down and then this girl's face awash in the mirror, swishing and crumpling.

I thought to my face in the mirror, What's wrong with me? Do I smell? Have bad breath? Am I so uninteresting? So awful?

I thought of Colin in the car. 'We mustn't keep the Professor's daughter out too late.' I thought, It's this damn house. Nobody would want to come here; it's like a morgue. Father locked in his study with his bloody books, Mary and her bloody friends. I thought, I'll get a flat. I'll go and live on my own in a flat. That should be better.

ℒ 5 ℒ

'Love,' said the carrot-haired student lying across my bed, 'Love is a compromised battleground. The young hurtle about on it clashing their fine, strong weapons and shouting war cries at each other. Only the old come slowly, carrion-picking over the fields, proclaiming vanished victories.'

'Aha,' I said.

'So what about truth then?' I said. First Love, then Truth.

'Truth,' said this student, 'truth is all the grey bits in between the things we hate and love most. Truth is the stubbing of your toe on the way to the bathroom to commit suicide.'

I got up to make coffee. We could go on like this for hours.

This is really living, I thought. My own flat, a student dropping in in the evening talking about Love and Truth.

Mary and my father hadn't seemed too surprised when I said I wanted to move into a flat of my own. Mary's jolly friend had said to her, 'Oh it's all the rage for young people nowadays.' That had been enough to convince her. Mary always made decisions like that; she'd hear somebody saying something on Woman's Hour on the BBC, or read an article in a magazine, or her friend would say, 'It's all the rage,' Mary would say, All right.

I found the flat through the students' accommodation officer at College. The student who had it had to go back to England.

Her mother was dying. The rent was two pounds, ten a week. Father said he'd pay it. The College gave me a raise. That gave me six pounds, ten a week to live on.

Mary gave me a desk and an old electric kettle and made curtains for the main room. My first Sunday there she and Father came for tea. I made queen cakes and we were all rather embarrassed. Mary kept saying, 'Well now, you look real comfy here.'

The first few weeks in the flat had been quite frightening. Evenings seemed incredibly long. I used to sit at the window and watch people walking along the canal: men with dogs, stiff men chucking their dogs' leads and uttering curt orders to them—some men can't leave their dogs alone; old-age pensioners who'd sit on benches for hours, transfixed by the weight of the years they'd lived and the few still to go, terrified of sputtering out—you'd want to shout out to them: *Get up, dance, make love, booze, go out with a bang!*—but they'd just sit there with their frozen faces. As soon as spring started into summer the children would come. Skinny, white-ribbed children with skinny dogs, all of them shouting and barking and the kids jumping into the dirty canal water. The kids would whistle and shout 'Hello there young one' if you went out. They were really old kids, workers' kids.

In February, I met this student. He came into the library office one day to explain to Miss Gore-Browne why he hadn't returned a particular book yet. She was out. He came back the next day and asked if I would like a cup of coffee. We started going round together, to the film society and the drama society. Things like that. I used to tell myself I quite liked him and listened to him attentively. Really I think I felt he was better than nothing, so I must have pitied him too.

This was a Saturday. I was making coffee and looking out the window at the canal. From so high you couldn't see the old bicycle frames and tin cans sticking in the muddy edges.

I shouted through, 'The canal is like a sleeping prostitute, all gaudy and gay and well-used.'

I looked round the door to see how he was reacting. 'Umh?' he said. He was squeezing a pimple.

Even that didn't deter. 'Life,' I said to myself, 'is a mixture of the sublime and the ridiculous.' That term we all spoke in clichés.

The student's name was Ian, only he spelt it Iain, to be different. I felt sorry for him thinking that one 'i' made him different. Iain was English. His mother was a writer for slick magazines and his father was a financier of something or other. They were terribly rich. They had a house in County Cork where they used to spend a couple of months a year, in winter, so's the father could hunt.

I was planning to go to bed with Iain. I didn't find him all that attractive, I just thought, Well he's someone I could go to bed with. It was a sort of revenge. He liked me more than I liked him. Before it had been the other way round. I used to link his arm sometimes in the street, hoping Colin would pass by and see us. I hadn't seen Colin for six weeks, or heard from him.

Iain's mother had come up to Dublin. We met her in the Shelbourne Hotel for coffee. She said I should come down to their house in Cork for a Hunt Ball. She said I must come down. She took me over. Iain said, 'You'll hate it,' but she'd taken him over long ago.

I was met off the Dublin train by Iain and his father. Iain had gone ahead. His father said in this loud braying voice, 'Aha! So here's the famed Miss O'Sullivan.' Everyone on the platform looked round. Then he clicked up porters to carry my weekend case. He was always clicking at people—clicking at porters, and waiters, and servants. I wondered did he click at his wife in bed when he wanted to make love to her.

Valerie once went to bed with a man who kept saying 'Just a little more to the left ... no, a little to the right now.' She said it was as if he were teeing up on a golf course. She said, 'I suppose you're aiming for a hole in one.' He didn't think it funny.

This family house was like an art gallery. The house was completely unlived-in, untouched. It existed apart, quite separately from its inhabitants. It was a house on display, showing itself discreetly and keeping its essence completely to itself. I was given a bedroom with a bathroom attached. The bathroom had two plaster busts of someone who looked like Caesar in a picture in our Latin books, and four gilt-edged mirrors. The mirrors watched, elegant and mocking, while I bathed, pouring half a bottle of foaming bubbly in on top, pretending I was Sophia Loren or somebody.

Iain's two sisters were over on holiday from London. In London they worked for advertising agencies. They tore around Cork in their father's Jaguar looking for antiques and laughing at the Irish. 'The Irish,' they'd say. 'Aren't they extraordinary!', making a 'straw' sound in the middle of 'extraordinary', and then they'd shriek with laughter.

The night of the Hunt Ball one of them came into my bedroom when I was dressing and said, 'We're going soon, you'd better hurry up and get out of that dressing gown.' I said, 'It's not a dressing gown, it's my dress.' Mary had lent it to me for the occasion. She said I'd be the Toast of County Cork in it. Iain's sister said, 'You'd better borrow one of my dresses,' flinging open her wardrobe and saying, 'Now, take anything you want,' then turning back the cupboard door showing me shelves of make-up and perfumes and saying, 'Borrow anything you want from here as well. But hurry up.'

I picked a long green and purple silk dress that hissed when I walked. Everyone said, 'You look marvellous.'

Iain and his father wore red hunting jackets because they were a hunting family. The father was once a Master. The sisters both had boyfriends over from London as well and they wore black velvet jackets and floppy silk cravats. Iain said you couldn't be seen dead in a monkey suit.

There were about two hundred people at the ball. The men were all in dinner jackets, the women in long silks and satins, with powdered faces and bright bloody lips and small earrings.

Down each side of the ballroom there was a long table covered in heavy white linen cloths and laid out with glasses and hundreds of knives and forks. The polished dance floor was in the middle and at the top end, seated up on a stage, was the band, 'The Starlight'; they were all from Cork.

It was hard to imagine how clean and stately the ballroom had looked when about four hours later men and women had put on paper hats and were dancing round and round the floor, the women clinging to the men as if they were drowning. The women's faces were no longer bright and bloody; they looked as if they'd been punched. The men were red in the face and clapping each other on the backs and the women on their behinds, saying 'Tallyho there, tallyho.' You'd have thought all these very respectable middle-class people in Cork with neat detached homes and clean children had gone quite mad.

Everyone drank champagne and it flowed up behind my head, and made my eyes alternately loose and tight. Iain said I didn't seem to be enjoying it; his face looked quite mean suddenly. I thought, 'He's getting his own back because he likes me more than I do him.' Then this girl from College with blonde curly hair came up and asked Iain to dance, and off they went. I thought, Of course I'm enjoying it. I'm just rather frightened.

I wished Colin were there. He'd laugh at them; he'd say, 'Quick, look at this woman over here with the duck's disease,' and point to a woman with a very low-slung bottom, or he'd say, 'How about old Head-the-Ball?' and that would be a Major or someone. He'd make you feel a spectator and you wouldn't be scared of Iain's sisters or his mother or the clicking father any more.

But Colin wasn't there. He was off somewhere. Off with beautiful girls. You'd seen them at College and at the television station. Girls with their legs brazen and long and their hair uncombed and tossed and their eyes looking and challenging, ready to go to bed with the men just for the hell of it.

One of the sisters' boyfriends leaned over and said, 'Men prefer blondes,' and gave me a wink, and said I looked a million miles away, and could he have the immense pleasure of the next dance. We danced then for quite a long time and he kissed my neck and said he was sure that beneath my cool exterior a passionate woman was trying to get out. I said, 'Oh really.' His remark annoyed me.

Then one of the sisters threw a chop bone at an old boyfriend across the room because she was a bit drunk and very loud, and the chop bone hit one of the waiters. The waiter picked up a glass of champagne and emptied it over her head. She screamed and Iain's father and a friend jumped up and grabbed the waiter by his elbows and frogmarched him out of the room. The waiter was grinning—he must have waited a long time for the pleasure. Everyone was very shocked—'The cheek of the bloody man!' They almost said 'native'. I thought, Up the Irish and the waiter, and damn the lot of you.

On the way out we had our pictures taken by an enterprising man who'd turned up at two in the morning with a Polaroid camera and a duffle coat. I still have the picture somewhere. Everyone is leaning slightly to one side with smiles stretched over their strained faces. One of the girls has a long wine stain down the front of her dress.

When we got home from the dance we all had a whiskey in the big echoing drawing room. Everyone was quieter. I wasn't frightened any more. The parents went up to bed and one of the sisters put on a record. Iain and I started dancing. He had a spot on the back of his neck. He said, 'Let's go and make some coffee.' We went outside and he pushed me up against the wall and started kissing me, wet kisses. That went on for a while then I got bored. Finally I said I was going up to bed. My head was beginning to hurt. Everything smelt of smoke: my hair, my clothes; my mouth tasted of it. I went in and ran a bath in the bathroom with the mirrors and the busts of Caesar. I turned the lights off and got in. It was like a midnight swim, the water holding you up and knowing it could so easily suck you down—deceptive, velvet water.

I wrapped one of the big towels round me and went back and lay on my bed. The bath and the whiskey. Warm inside and out.

The door opened with a slice of light. Iain came in. He was wearing silk pyjamas. They made me laugh. 'Shh', he whispered. He sat on the edge of the bed. He had two cups of coffee. We lit up cigarettes. The kissing downstairs seemed a long time ago. A regrettable time. I wished Iain would go. He got into bed beside me. He said he was cold. We finished our coffee in silence.

Iain's thing was like a cold, raw sausage. I was holding it in my hand and hoping it would stiffen for him. We were sort of rolling round in the bed. Like people trying to get comfortable. Iain was kissing me and saying, 'I love you,' and my head had suddenly cleared like the sky on a spring day—one minute there are clouds, the next the wind whishes through and everything is quite clear and washed. I was thinking of seagulls. Somewhere I'd read that they have to nap and beat their wings and sit screaming at each other for hours in order to make themselves sufficiently excited to manage sexual intercourse.

After about an hour I told Iain he'd better go. What would his mother say if she came in in the morning?—it would be worse than finding him in bed with the maid. So we didn't see so much of each other when we got back to Dublin.

≈ 6 ≈

The girl in Valerie's boutique had forgotten me. 'I tried on a red dress one day,' I said, 'And you said I should take up modelling.' The girl was busy; a new consignment of clothes had just arrived. She said, 'Just a minute then.' It was lunchtime. The boutique was closed. Valerie made us all some coffee. I thought, Why did I come? She probably says that to everyone.

I told Valerie about the dance in County Cork. She said, 'It sounds really brutal.' I said it was that, *brutal*. She said, 'How's the old love life then?' and flipped her eyes at me. I said, 'So so.' I said this madly rich Englishman was desperately in love with me, *but*. 'But what?' said Valerie. 'Oh I don't know,' I said, 'I find him rather boring.' I hadn't seen Iain for a week; he was the rich Englishman.

It was a Saturday morning. The canal was silky from the sun. I was sitting in the flat and reading an article in a magazine about a model in London. She said she made a hundred pounds per photographic session. There were pictures of her in smart restaurants with Italian-looking men; there were pictures of her in very clean, pretty bras and pants making her face up at a beautiful dressing table with a *broderie anglaise* frill; there were pictures of her doing her modelling, lips pushed forward, hand on her hip, head thrown back, hair blowing. The girl said, 'Modelling can really change your life. You don't have to be beautiful to do it—just know how to make the best of yourself.'

I thought of that girl in the boutique. She said I should try modelling. If it changed my life it was worth trying then, wasn't it? I put on my best clothes and walked down to the boutique to ask her what I should do. Here I was and she couldn't remember me.

She was standing in the middle of piles of clothes, coffee in one hand, pencil in the other. 'Ah yes, now I remember—the hamstrung.' 'The what?' I said. 'The hamstrung,' said the girl, 'we nicknamed the dress that because of the lacing.' I said, 'It reminded me of tennis shoes.' She didn't say anything; she just looked at me as if to say, For heaven's sake, look what the cat's brought in.

I thought, There's many a slip … and I thought of a nun at school who used to say it: 'There's many a slip 'twixt cup and the lip.' I asked her once what it meant. She said, 'For instance, if a man were jumping off a bridge, committing suicide, between the decision to jump and the long fall down to when he hit the water, he might change his mind. He might decide he didn't want to die after all. Of course,' said this nun, 'Of course it would be too late for the body to be saved but never too late for the soul. We can be sure that the good God would forgive such a man—even at the last minute.' I was haunted by that man for weeks afterwards. I could see his tortured, grey face and him plummeting like a knife to the cold river saying, 'Oh no, no, no …'

The girl said 'Yes.' She was looking through a notebook. 'Here it is.' She handed me a black card with gold lettering. The lettering said Suzanna's School of Charm. It gave an address and a telephone number. I looked at the card. I said 'Thank you very much.' I looked at the card again, then at Valerie, then at the girl. The girl broke out laughing; the sound came out like a vase cracking. 'You really are a little greenhorn aren't you?' she said. 'If you want to be a model, kiddo, then you've got to take a modelling course. This card is the card of a modelling school. Maybe they'll accept you.' She was savage and sad, this girl; she'd laugh at you then give you a hand up again.

She said she knew Suzanna, the girl who ran the modelling school. She'd ring her up and make an appointment for me. I said, 'Yes, thank you, yes.' I wished and wished I hadn't started this whole damn business. I wished I'd gone shopping with Mary, or walking, or anything.

The girl spoke to Suzanna. She said a young dolly friend of hers wanted to try a bit of modelling; she said, 'Yes, she's not bad, a bit gauche but a good figure, long legs … yes, okay, fine, tutty bye now … byeee.'

I was to go over right away. I walked out into the street and started towards this School of Charm. When I looked at that model girl that morning I said to myself, If I looked like that I'd be both irresistible and invulnerable. Colin would be bound to find me irresistible. I would walk into him one day with my sexy hips and haughty face and wham he would go, flat on his knees and say, 'I adore you' and so on. There's another thing: I want to be richer, not rolling in money, but have money enough to be able to walk into the smartest shops and not feel I have to buy something because the sales girls would think I was poor. If I were a model, making a hundred pounds per photographic session, things would definitely improve. I mean, if I knew that a hundred pounds an hour was actually what I was worth, it would give me a lot of confidence. I'd look at all those damn girls in the College and think, Well I'm worth so much and that's that.

Suzanna sat behind a pale cream-coloured desk wearing pale cream-coloured clothes, her thick curly hair foaming round her face. It was just a question of knowing how to make the best of yourself.

I filled in a form. I didn't know my height, or weight, or waist, or hips or bust. I always bought 34B bras and mostly they fitted. She had a little pair of scales in her office. Off with the shoes and overcoat and onto the scales. 'Mmh,'—she wasn't pleased— 'You'll have to lose about a stone,' she said. 'Cut out bread, potatoes and sweet things.' She measured my bust and waist and hips. She put me up against the wall and registered my height. It all went neatly into the form. She said, 'Come back next Saturday morning for some photographic tests—let's hope you'll have lost a bit of that puppy fat by then, mmh?' Her phone rang. I was dismissed. I gathered up my shoes, my coat, my bag, my magazine. I went out into the street.

I stood for a minute—weighed and measured, charted and taped. You were a definable, defined, material substance. You had limits. You lived in the limit of your human skin; it weighed down onto the ground. You were rooted to the ground by that weight. You were limited by your edges to other edges. You were isolated and totally imprisoned. You wanted to scream.

I went into a bookshop and bought a book on 'How to Slim the Easy Way'. It measured out cupful after cupful of carrot and cabbage and mince and fillet steak and double cream, by calorific value. It had pictures too. Your life stretched before you in cups, white delft cups like the ones at school, full of raw and protein foods.

By the next Saturday I'd lost five pounds. 'Good,' said Suzanna, 'you look better already. Don't you feel better?' I said I did. I felt awful. The book gave a diet of poached eggs and tomatoes; it was the cheapest diet they listed. The others were king prawns without olive oil dressing, or fillet steak without peperone sauce. The poached eggs sat in my tummy gaseous with reproach.

I was brought into another room. There were five other girls there—potential models.

The make-up expert, Miss Gilligan, came in. 'All make-up, false eyelashes, wigs, etcetera, off please. Then line up along this wall.' She might have been one of those Nazi women. Giggling we stripped and scrubbed and lined up. We smiled at each other and sized each other up. Miss Gilligan walked along the line looking at each one of us. She stopped by a tall girl beside me; *Trrrp, trrrp,* she went and whipped the girl's eyelashes off—'I thought we said all falsies off, dear?' The girl wept. Miss Gilligan took notes.

The poise expert, Miss O'Halloran, came in. She had a pretty clown's face, funny-sad. She asked each of us to walk up and down the room. Then to stoop and pretend to pick something up off the floor. Then to sit down. We each thought the other awful.

The photographer came in. He was introduced to us. He was called Tom. He had a very humble-looking face which meant he was probably very arrogant. He called us 'ducky' as he got to know us better. He was Suzanna's lover.

The course was to take four weeks—a crash course. It was to cost forty pounds. We were to arrive at the School at 8.00 a.m., we would bring our lunches with us, we would be free to go at 5.00 p.m.; however, most evenings we would have some sort of talk from a former model or beautician or health expert. The course would not, of course, make us professional models, but it would be a start. 'The start is the thing in this game, as in any other game,' said Suzanna. Suzanna's school was also an agency; that is, once we'd finished the course, our photograph, name, bust, waist, hips, height, weight and 'personality' would be filed in a large album that Suzanna kept on her desk. Then the men from the advertising agencies would come in and thumb through the albums trying to match their product, to our faces, to somebody else's catchline. We all bravely smiled and pouted out from the celluloid scrap book, asking to be bought.

I went to the College and asked Miss Gore-Browne for my holidays. She agreed. I asked Mary to lend me forty pounds. She agreed. Mary was delighted; she said, 'Come round and let us see the developments.'

Each day was broken up into three sessions: Poise and Personality session; Deportment and General Health session; Make-up and Dress session. Each teacher shared a common technique; the technique was to make us thoroughly and shamefully aware of our long-neglected, weedy, overgrown bodies; of our under-nourished, undercleansed, under-toned skin; of our sloppy walk; our unhandy methods; our ungraceful gestures; our unshaven legs and hairy armpits; of our broken nails and rough hands, and on and on until we broke down and handed our bodies over to them to re-make. We wondered how we had survived so long in such ignorance of the tasks of beautiful women.

'My God!' Miss Gilligan, the make-up expert, would say, peering at your skin. 'My God!' You would cringe and cower and think, 'Christ, what has she seen?' She'd stand back for a minute, run her fingers through her hair. Then peer down again. This was obviously a Most Difficult Case. You would feel awful. A failure. A failure as a woman. Your skin was a pig's back. *Oh dear God, I'm sorry for not having nicer skin.*

She would give you a last minute reprieve. 'With the greatest care and attention,' she would say, 'I think we can just about salvage this skin.' You would want to fling yourself at her feet, kiss them, say 'Thank you, thank you.'

She would say that the three rules for the face are these: cleanse, tone and nourish; cleanse, tone and nourish; cleanse, tone and nourish—you'd chant them going home in the bus, and walking down the street, and up the stairs to your flat: *cleanse, tone and nourish.*

The poise expert, Miss O'Halloran, made us act out charades of how to behave in certain situations. 'The model girl's artifices do not stop at her face and physical appearance,' Miss O'Halloran would say. 'Oh no. Being a model is a way of life.' (A way of life? A way to change your life? A million, million ways?)

Miss O'Halloran's favourite charade was called 'Going to the Restaurant'. There were two actors: the Escort, and his Escortee, the Little Lady.

The Escort would stand looking at his (her) watch, evening paper tucked under his arm, whistling gently. Some minutes would pass. A benevolent smile would be fixed on the Escort's face. Ten minutes. 'Tsch, tsch. Women are such battery creatures,' the beaming gentleman would say.

Then. With a trot and a skip, in would come the Little Lady. Smiling and waving and 'Oh Lord, am I *ever so* late?' He would say, 'Of course not.'

The Escort would suggest a place to go and eat. The Little Lady would tremulously and immediately agree, 'Oh, that would be soopa!' The Escort would hail a cab.

The Escort would open and close all doors, the Little Lady

would swish through. At one stage she would turn and show us the contents of her neat little bag—waterproof cosmetic case, comb, atomizer, spare nylons, and a little cash—just in case.

The Little Lady would behave like a little dumb idiot the whole time, allowing the Escort to lead her to a table, pull out her chair, choose her food, order it for her, order the wine, and order the conversation. If the Escort said, 'The moon is made of cream caramel, lightly spiced with caraway seeds,' the Little Lady would open her wide eyes wider and say, 'Oh really?'

The Escort would, of course, pay for everything. That's what Escorts are for.

Our lives became circumspect, structured. Entering a room was not simply a question of opening the door and walking in; it entailed Creating a Presence, Moving with Ease and Dignity, and so on. Leaving a room was almost as difficult; it meant getting out of the door without turning your back, or your Presence, on the company.

Miss O'Halloran said to us: 'Now girls, remember what Samuel Goldwyn, that doyen and genius of Hollywood, used to say to his women—beautiful women: "Ladies, if you want to be devastating use all the arts of sophistication available, but remain *demure*." You must learn to seduce and make the victim think he's enjoying it.'

The four weeks went by in a frenzy of bashing of fatty flesh to break down fatty tissue, twirling ankles in the air, twisting necks, swivelling eyes, scraping skins down and dressing them up, entering and exiting. Becoming models. (I read a book one night that said, 'We cry and we enter—that's life. We cry and we exit— that's death.' I thought it pretty stupid. The main thing was all the crying in between.)

One girl couldn't take the pace. She left, white-faced, with her cosmetic case tucked under her arm.

'Smile,' said the photographer. 'Come on then, ducky, give us a nice big smile.' We learnt how to smile, pout, look frightened, look lustful, look baby-doll. Smiling was the most important of all. Right round the school there were pictures of girls smiling; not the kind of smiles we'd done before—I'm-going-to-burst-with-laughter-any-minute. No. Dimpled smiles, coy smiles, wide smiles, sexy smiles.

Knowing smiles were the only taboo kind. Knowing anything, worse still showing it, was pretty taboo. All you had to know was how to sell yourself. In fact the agency would do that for you.

The first job the agency got for me was doing a simple fashion show for the Irish Countrywomen's Association. They were having a dinner and the new secretary had thought a little fashion parade would be 'good fun for the girls'. The 'girls' were mostly in their forties and had worn the same things since they were in their thirties.

Suzanna sent myself and another girl called Trish to do the show. Trish had quite a plain face but sensational legs. Sunbeam had once asked her to model their stockings at the Dublin Spring Show. She'd been sitting up on this display stand with all the hosiery and woollen goods, and only her legs were visible through this sort of cardboard laurel wreath affair. She had to sit there for four hours every day with her legs on display. She said it was suffocating behind the curtain. One day a big farmer from Kerry came up to the stand. She could hear him having an argument about the legs with another farmer. Were they real or were they not? 'Yirra get on outta that,' said the farmer and grabbed at Trish's legs. He knocked her off her stool, the curtain fell down, the laurel wreath fell down and there was Trish amidst the debris saying 'Ya big bloody eejit' to the farmer who was puce with the shock already. Trish had a terrible temper if she wanted to use it.

Well. The first job for me was a bit of a disaster. Trish was quite calm and walked up and down the little stage in tweed skirts and smiled at the women. I was terribly nervous and couldn't remember what I was supposed to say about each costume and tore one of the dresses. The women were very polite and clapped at the end of it and said we must have the dinner with them. One of them said we were like 'young fillies, graceful young fillies with your long legs and shining manes'. The other women looked embarrassed beside her.

We spent the night in a bed and breakfast place. Fifteen bob each. Our room had four beds: one double, three single, and five china chamber pots.

After that things got better.

∽ 7 ∽

The discotheque had only been open a week. The jet set still felt obliged to be there. Next week, next month, it would be somewhere else. Everyone knew everyone else. Everyone sat around in their expensive clothes, eating expensive food, unable to hear a word anyone was saying because of the pop music which was blaring out of two enormous speakers and filling the blackness of the tiny rooms. Everyone was laughing big bright orange laughs and thinking, Wow, we're having a great time, really great. That's if they thought at all.

Suddenly I saw Colin. He was sitting the far side of the floor to us with a girl. I felt my face going hot. The man I was with was going on and on about some 'terrible orgy' he'd been to the night before and what I'd missed and blah, blah, blah.

I said, 'Excuse me just a minute.' I got up and walked slowly over to Colin's table. I said 'Hello' and 'How *are* you' quite loudly to some people nearby and bent over their table; then I saw him looking. I pretended to be so surprised—'Well, fancy meeting you here, Colin!' (You'll never know how I waited and hurt and plotted. I'm a friendly friend, pleased, of course, to see you.)

Colin had half got up. 'Well Liz, I say, ehm, this is…'

I said, 'Oh, so this is the latest?' and smiled at the girl. Oh the innocence of innocent women—let them all suffer, why should I care? Colin said the girl's name and he introduced me as an old friend and you could see him looking and thinking, She's looking pretty good. I said, 'Anyway, don't let me interrupt you,' with an emphasis on interrupt. 'Here's my card—drop in sometime, when you feel like it.' I handed him a card. Suzanna had told us to have some made; it looked more professional. Mine had 'Liz' written in long spidery letters and then my address and the address of the agency at the bottom.

David, the man I was with, was sulky when I got back. 'Who was that?' he said.

I felt like glass, like spun sugar—I felt I could shout, or never say anything again.

I said, 'Oh, just an old friend. Two old friends.' Simple. David said the food was getting cold. I said, 'Who cares about the bloody old food?' He whined, 'Oh Lizzie, I don't know what's got into you tonight.' 'So far,' I said, 'nothing.' David groaned. His mother had told him, among a million other things, that Nice Girls were never vulgar. David's mother didn't really think there were such creatures as Nice Girls, at least not nice enough for her little David. She would let you know as soon as you met her.

David weighed fifteen stone. He was a property speculator. He bought his suits in London and wore wide silk ties and a red carnation on special occasions. He had this wide and very soft face. A face like a crab's, white, with beady eyes well out to the side.

David and I had met at a party Suzanna gave at the school and agency. We'd often go to dinner after parties. He was always putting his hand on my knee under the table.

David was the first person, of my own age group, whom I met who'd made a lot of money. He was fantastically vulgar with his money, always trying to impress people with it. It made him almost vulnerable. He would buy me presents and send round great wobbling bunches of flowers with stiff little messages on them. At first I used to feel guilty about all the presents. Trish said, 'Don't be such a bloody idiot—if he weren't spending it on you he'd be spending it on somebody else, so what's the difference? Anyway, he probably regards it as an investment—"fifteen dinners in the Shelbourne and *then* will you come to bed with me?"' Trish could be tough as nails. Trish said, 'Oh bugger off, I came up the hard way.'

If I smiled and laughed at David he would say, 'Happy Girl'; if I went mopey he'd say, 'Who's a Lonely Heart today?' and put his arm around me. It was nice to have someone who said those things just to you—somebody watching your emotions and saying yes or no. He used to say 'You're my dark Rosaleen Liz' and 'I love you.' It was comforting.

He wanted me to come and live with him, even though he was terrified his mother might find out. He was thirty-five. He'd only moved out of home the year before. I said no. I wasn't quite sure why. I said yes, I'd go to bed with him. He used to like us to go to bed together on Saturdays and then spend Sunday at his flat. It was very regular.

One night we came in very late. David was quite drunk; we'd been at a champagne party. He put on a black silky slip of mine. He stuck a carnation in his hair. He started prancing in front of the mirror. The slip was made of this stretch nylon and it was pulled across his chest with hair coming out through the cleavage. We were both roaring laughing. Then he threw himself on the bed and said, 'Come and sit on top of me.' He'd gone very quiet. I was quiet too, frightened (if the nuns could see me now), and I was sitting astride him and he had his eyes closed and was moaning.

I'd nearly laugh out loud sometimes watching David with his friends talking business. Serious, and jaw, jaw. I'd think of him in that damn slip and wonder, are they like that? And everything would seem just a tiny veneer of manners and clothes over this mad chaos.

I can't remember what we all talked about. None of David's friends ever read books. They had jobs in advertising, or marketing, or property firms. 'Life,' they'd say, 'is a Big Joke.' If you didn't laugh 90 per cent of the time you were with them they'd think you were dying of heartbreak or something. They'd sit in pubs, their bottoms filling onto the seats and stretched into their trousers. They'd shout at the barman for more drinks and slap their fat, tight thighs. At Easter they'd go to the races and stand round in the beer tent going, Ha ha. They'd go to hotels and restaurants with their girlfriends and the girlfriends would laugh as well, but dropping their eyes and watching. They'd all say goodnight to each other, shouting 'Goodnight' across the street and slamming their car doors, still laughing.

The girlfriends all pretended to be bosom pals. You couldn't even go to the loo on your own without one of them rushing in after you. It was all giggles and 'That's a beautiful dress you have on' and behind that hate. I hate you and damn your dress and your sexy figure and your smile.

We were supposed to meet for coffees the day after and scheme and chatter and talk about who wore what, and who was sleeping with whom, and go and have our hair done together. We were The Girls. The boyfriends would say to us, all indulgence and fat grins, 'And where have you girls been?', like you would ask children. We didn't trust each other for one minute; all the time we were looking and watching with big smiles stuck over our faces.

It was a spring and summer of a new life. It was modelling bras and a new soap powder and clothes at the boutique. Suzanna said I didn't work hard enough at it. She meant I didn't sleep with all the right people and go to all the right places. She said, 'You'll never get to the top unless you give your whole self to it.'

The world opened up a bit and there were lots more people suddenly and things to be done and places to go to, this place or that, wherever the fancy took you. You were buying clothes and painting the flat and going to dinner parties and discotheques.

The world opened up a bit but closed a bit as well. I saw this scientific picture. It was about white mice. Scientists were studying the white mice to see if it could tell them something about human beings. The mice lived in connecting cages. If a male mouse, say, saw some female mouse that he really fancied he could go running through this little connecting door and find her in the next one. The horrible part about it was he couldn't get out again. He could never get back to his original cage— only on to another one, and another one. I hated that feeling— forfeiting one experience for another. So. The world opened a bit and closed a bit.

At night when it was dark and you were the only one awake you'd think about your life, your young life, and about your looks. Mostly about your looks.

We were the little dancers on the stage; puppets dressed in the shortest skirts and the deepest *décolletés* and the tightest jeans.

We danced and danced to please and flatter and titivate and charm. The hand that pushed and pulled us might jerk us right off the stage or drop us, so we had to keep going. We danced till our limbs ached and our faces felt stiff and all the time we were wondering, *Am I okay? Does he really fancy me? Is my bosom sexier than hers? Is my bottom too flat? Are my eyes nice? Have I passed the test again? Am I okay, okay, okay?*

Modelling had helped you in that way. The other girls would say, 'Oh for God's sake, no need to get so upset,' and you learnt from them how to be a bit blasé and walk with your bosom stuck out and your hips moving. You knew you, for the moment, were part of the crowd. You knew you were good looking by their standards at least. You could walk into restaurants and bars and parties and keep your face blank and your head blank and know men were looking at you, and you thought, Fine, just fine.

You didn't know what you were yourself. You'd stopped thinking, worrying about that.

∽ **8** ∽

Colin rang the agency and left a message for me: 'Old friend coming to see you. Tuesday at seven.' I thought, I knew he'd come, but I hadn't known at all. I went out and bought these very tight black trousers that I'd seen in Valerie's place.

The first thing he said when he came into the flat was, 'So, the Professor's daughter grows up, tunes in, and turns on.' He was laughing, his eyes taking in the flat, the furniture, me. You could see he was thinking, Well she's doing okay for herself anyway.

I poured us a drink—a large whiskey for him, an orange juice for me. I put on a record; my hand was wobbling. Bach's concerto fluted out into the room. Colin was sitting on an old chesterfield sofa that David and I had bought down at the quays. Chesterfield sofas were all the rage.

We both said, 'Well' together and then laughed, little pools of silence eddying and sucking between floating conversation. I thought, Don't panic, relax. I thought, You're a woman in her flat, surrounded by her possessions. I thought, There's you and there's

Colin and you're having a conversation. That is all.

Valerie used to tell us at school that when somebody really intimidates you, you should think of them sitting on the lav; she said once you think of somebody on the lav they won't scare you any more. We used to work it on the nuns.

Colin was saying, 'Well I suppose you're making pots of money now—since you've taken up the modelling business.' I told him I didn't do all modelling. I'd kept the job in the library part time (security?); I said, 'The photographer I work with is a queer; well not really a queer but completely asexual.' I hadn't even thought of it before. Why did I say it? Colin said something about girls liking queers because they don't feel threatened by them. Wrong again, this one would burn the eyes out of you with jealousy, envy.

I asked him how the Fir Bolgs were. He said fine. His programmes were due to start in the autumn schedule. He'd had some trouble with the Civil War sections. Too many people still alive from that period, all with different points of view. I thought of a big garbage can with everyone picking and picking.

He said, 'You weren't very nice to that girl the other night.'

'Me? Not nice? Oh, how?' (How can a Nice Girl not be nice?)

'It doesn't matter.'

I said, 'Well of course it does.' We smiled. Almost conspirators.

He said we should go on a pub crawl round the docks area. Where the workers drink. 'I think you should see how the other half lives,' he said, 'for a wee change.' That night I was not noticing sarcasm.

The phone rang. It was David, wanting to come round. 'I'm tired, going to have an early night,' I said. 'No, I'm going to bed almost immediately. No please don't come David, I'd honestly prefer to be on my own—yes, honestly. Yes. I'll give you a tinkle tomorrow at the office. Bye now, byeee.'

Colin was laughing, his hand over his mouth. 'So that's how it's done!—the Brush Off?'

'I *am* tired,' I said. Pompous. Damn David. Damn him blind.

We walked down along the canal. Colin left his car parked outside the flat. It was cold. In winter you could feel the air cracking and stiffening with the cold. This summer air was calm, but still cold. The sky was very high and suspended, as if it might blow off.

Colin said, 'Your nose is pink,' and then said, 'Don't worry, it makes you look less like you've just walked out of a magazine.'

That was always the pattern with him from then on. Making remarks about your nose being red, or that colour looking poxy on you, and then he'd laugh and link your arm and say, 'C'mon then Lizzie, I was only joking.' You'd say, 'Mmm', and give a little laugh, but stay wondering inside.

We went to this pub on the quays where a sailor had been knifed the night before. One of the Dockers told Colin. It was called 'The Twilight'. It was bright like a dentist's room. The walls were yellow with cardboard pictures hung around of ships balanced on huge seas. Bottles were piled like Skittles behind the barman's head.

They were all men except for two women with dyed hair in the snug. The women were drinking half pints and smoking cigarettes. One had her slippers on. The men wore donkey jackets. They put their hands right round their pints of Guinness and looked down into their glasses when they drank.

Colin was greeted by the barman with a wink: 'A pint I suppose, is it, Mr Dempsey.' The barman knew him. 'An' what will it be for the lady?' he said. Colin said 'A half pint' before I'd time to say anything. I said, 'I don't drink Guinness, actually.' A few of the men near us turned round. They looked at me, then Colin. 'Bejay, Colin, and how's the head, uh?' They were slapping hands and saying, 'Jaysus, now, and how's things?' Colin said, 'Grand.' Then he put his arm around me and said, 'And this is Elizabeth O'Sullivan.' He paused. 'A model,' he said.

One of the men said, 'A what?' and there was a big shout of laughter. They all nodded their heads and some of them shook hands with me. Colin said, 'I thought I'd bring her down to see how the other half lives.' The men laughed again. 'Pearl amongst swine,' said one of them, and grinned at me.

We went to three more pubs. I was drinking Bacardi and Coke. Colin said, 'Oh the real Dublin bourgey drink.'

I said, 'I don't understand.'

'The drink for all the clean-living ladies out to live it up and find men for themselves.'

In each pub Colin knew people. He was talking and laughing and buying drinks and introducing me, then linking arms, we'd be away to the next one. He said that in the first pub I looked as if I thought the men were going to bite me.

In the third pub I asked where the ladies' was. The barman said, 'The wha'?' 'The Ladies',' I said, 'you know—the loo.'

This woman who was sitting in a corner in a crumpled tweed coat was called over. The barman had a whispered conversation with her. She said, 'Come with me, love.' We went up the back stairs of the pub and along a thin draughty corridor. She opened the fourth door on the left. 'In there love,' she said, 'I'll wait for ya.'

At first I couldn't see anything, just this empty room with a bed, bare boards, and the moonlight falling coldly in. Then the moonlight showed up this china chamber pot, right in the middle of the floor. I squatted over it. The pee wouldn't come for ages. It was like school—having to pee for the infirmary nun into a jar and the pee not coming for ages. You'd been bursting to go a minute before.

Colin said he was hungry. It was eleven o'clock. I was feeling this light, tight sensation all over. I started singing as we were walking back—a song from school—'Shine out great sun and brin-i-i-ing the day-a-a-a-ay.' It was a song for four parts and swept up and down like a swollen river, rising and falling. Colin was laughing and saying, 'More, more' and clapping his hands in the middle of the street. People looked at us and we chanted on.

We came to this café. Colin said, 'And now for some *déjeuner.*' He ordered bacon and eggs, twice, bread and tea, twice. I thought 'I'll diet tomorrow.' He said, 'Now stop worrying about your figure. You're beautiful.' He kissed the back of my hand and then turned it over and looked at the palm and started reading it. 'A long life … ever so long Missus … a fine, tall handsome stranger

… but oh what's this? Oh my, my.' I said, 'Stop. Please, stop.'

The café was full of people. There was a jukebox and these two scrubbers were standing in front of it. 'Scrubbers' is slang for factory girls. They were chewing gum and wiggling, and slapping their mouths open and shut with the gum in time to the music.

The floor of the café was covered in red tiles, all broken. Black and slimy where the cement floor showed through. There were cigarette burns on the plastic tops of the tables and all over the floor, like a disease.

On the counter there was a Perspex display box. Inside were slices of apple tart and cream crackers and angel cakes laid out on white paper doilies as if they'd been quietly left to expire. On the wall there was a big blackboard. It said: liver sausages, beans and chips 4/6d, tonight's speciality. Bread and tea were a shilling extra. Colin said he hadn't seen the board changed in a year.

You could eat either sitting up at the counter or down at a table. Men sat up at the counter and ogled the three women who ran the place. The biggest one was called Dolly. She had bright yellow hair, and the hairs stuck one by one out of this pink scalp, like a doll's. Colin said, 'She used to be a tart, but got a bit old for it.' Dolly would just say, *Oh neow* when the men passed remarks at her. Colin said she was as strong as a horse. One night she'd chucked a man out into the street because he'd got a bit uppity.

Then an oldish man came in, reeling, his clothes torn, a greasy hat on his head. He sat down near the two scrubbers and was dribbling and watching them. Suddenly two men came over, took him by one arm each and ran him out through the door. They came in again a few seconds later, fags in the corners of their mouths still, slapping their sleeves.

I was getting up, saying, 'Colin, we must help that poor old man, what are they doing to him?' Colin pulled me down. 'He was jacking himself off in front of the girls, you dope.'

Outside the café Colin tossed a coin. 'Heads my place, tails it's yours.' It was tails. I panicked. I thought of somebody in a play who said, 'The first step to wisdom is to stop. Whatever it is, stop it. Then maybe you'll find out.'

I said, 'Hang on a minute.' I thought, This isn't what I'd planned at all. I hadn't planned anything.

We walked back to my flat. Quieter. Colin lit a small fire when we got in. He poured us each a whiskey. He said, 'Drink up.' I went and quickly had a glass of milk in the kitchen. In the bathroom I sprayed on some deodorant, under the arms, between the legs. A drop of Gold Spot on the tongue. A touch of powder on the slightly shiny nose and chin—'danger areas, girls,' Miss Gilligan had said.

On your body there were *erogenous zones* and *danger areas* and *areas of temptation* and your *private parts*, like a survey map. They were all mixed up together and their values kept changing as you grew up. Your private parts were your personal bank account. You kept them for bartering with husbands or lovers —depending on whether you were a Catholic or not.

The nuns had said, 'Oh, the body is the source of many temptations,' but then when you grew up a bit people would say, 'Oh, the body is the source of all pleasure.' It was confusing. The pleasure and the temptations were tangled together.

I thought, I don't look too bad, considering.'

The fire came up slowly. Colin had put in three fire lighters and then stacked the sticks like a wigwam round them and then briquettes round the sticks. I put on a record. I thought, Everything is just right: music, a fire, a little drink, Colin. I thought, Let it stay. Stay for ever.

'You've grown up so much since I last met you,' Colin said. 'You look harder.' I thought, He doesn't like me. I knew it all along. Thinks I'm hard—am I hard? I don't feel hard inside.

He said, 'I've been thinking about you quite a bit you know. Since we last met.'

'Why didn't you ring me up and find out if I was thinking of you?' I said, brazen.

'I thought you were still living at home.'

'So?'

'So I didn't want to get involved and end up chastely kissing you goodnight on your father's doorstep every evening, terrified you were half an hour late.'

'How did that stop you seeing me?'

'Well you were hot for it, too, weren't you?' He gestured. 'Going out to cinemas and theatres every night isn't my idea of a relationship.'

You were hot for it, too. That had stopped me dead. You weren't supposed to say things like that—*hot for it*, like a bitch on heat. You certainly weren't supposed to say it like that. Spoiled, all spoiled.

Colin was talking again. Gently now, calming. 'Don't be hurt, we can be really good together Liz, you know that.' He was stroking my arm and his hand was touching my ear under my hair. 'I'd like to make love to you, right here in front of the fire.'

I got up. I thought, Oh, a little faint, Oh, inside myself. I said, 'That's a bit sudden, isn't it?' I thought, For God's sake your voice is going to break any minute.

Colin was patting the carpet beside him, tap, tap, and smiling. I was thinking, Fool, fool, you must make him work harder, you can't just throw yourself at him, remember the rules, relax, smile, pretend it's all in a day's work, you're only doing it for kicks—right?

'That's my girl,' Colin was saying, 'That's my girl,' and putting his drink down and pulling me down beside him and pushing me back and his mouth coming down and his eyes, covering, covering …

Then you were on the floor and it was like coming out from under an anaesthetic, one minute thinking *Oh come into me, fill me, touch me,* and then wondering if your hair would get burnt in the fire, getting the smell of the damn paraffin from the fire lighters; Colin's hands working up and down—he was like wire, his body like live wire between you, and you thought of all the women all over the world opening their legs like double doors for their men, opening and opening, and then you were wanting every hole in your body stopped up: your eyes, your mouth, your ears, your nose, and the gap between your thighs widening like a crack in an earth tremor, and you wanting deep, deep right inside and outside to let the whole world rattle the doors and rant and rave.

Colin left a note pinned to the bedsheet; it said he'd ring me during the day and tell me when he finished work and we'd go out for dinner together that evening. It said 'You were fantastic.' There was a drawing of a little man with a smiling face and a huge penis. Colin was always drawing things.

I went out and bought flowers. It was a public holiday. I sat on the bridge by the canal. I smiled at an old man whose coat was fastened with a pin——I thought, Oh the poor old people, how awful it must be to be old. But it made it even better to be young.

Oh bodies, I thought, who would have thought bodies could be like this? People noticed and looked. It's always like that—when you are dancing inside they'll look and appreciate and when you've been skulking and cringing along they almost bark at you as you pass by. Or is that all just in your head?

I had lunch with Valerie and told her I'd fallen in love. She said, 'Good luck, but be careful.' I laughed in her face with my strong, hot love.

At five o'clock Colin rang. His voice so different over the telephone. He said would I mind if he came round for a bath, my flat was nearer to town. The flowers went into the bathroom and bath oil and clean towels and I was shy, washing him and looking at his hair curling, wet on his neck and then we were both in the bath and throwing water and shouting and before we went out the woman below came up and said, 'I'd like ye to know me ceiling is wringing wet' and gave a poisonous look and Colin said, 'Well how about wringing it dry Missus?' and we leant against the door bursting laughing.

We went out to dinner. The restaurant had a special table for us with a candle and a little bowl of heather in the middle and the waiters knew Colin and one of them had a face like an owl and dry hands. He said he'd been a waiter since he was thirteen.

During dinner I don't remember what he said. What I said. I

remember his eyes, his brown-black eyes and this feeling of him all over me, all through me, touching his hand and feeling the touch spreading all over me. Rocking in his eyes and becoming beautiful and golden in the watchfulness of his eyes.

He said, 'Come to Galway with me for the weekend.' We were having liqueurs and cigars. He said, 'I've got to do a recording of traditional music in Spiddal.' He said we'd stay the night in a hotel in Galway, on the company's expenses; that I could come out and watch the recording session; that we could go down on the train and have lunch and a bottle of wine; that it might be quite fun. I was saying, 'Yes, yes I'd love to do that.'

I was thinking I'd write Suzanna a note saying my father was ill and to cancel any appointments for me for the weekend, and I'd write Miss Gore-Browne a note saying I was ill. And I'd write David a note saying I was going to visit an aunt in the country.

Colin was saying, 'It's simple—just follow your desires and to hell with what other people think of you. They can't eat you.' We composed them each a small note, enough to be going on with. Keep them at bay with white paper.

Suzanna would say—did say—'Well why jeopardize your career? You could be a very good model, you know, but you can't just run off whenever you want to and have dirty weekends in Galway.' I thought, Career, job, money, they're not important. I'll think about all that later.

That second night we went to Colin's flat. He said, 'We'll make love in three different places, three different nights. Variety is the spice of love.'

We were quieter then. He wanted the light on and he leaned on one elbow looking and barely touching and he kept his eyes open and he said, 'It's beautiful to see you come.' I felt frightened almost, exposed.

The following afternoon he picked me up in a taxi. He introduced me to Jilly, his production assistant, and Bill Summers, the cameraman. The rest of the crew was in Galway already. I wondered if he had slept with Jilly. She was tall and heavy with bad skin and curly brown hair; she was attractive in a defiant sort of way that said 'Look I know I don't look like a fashion model, but if you want me you can have me—and I won't thank you for it.'

On the train the three of them talked about the recording session and how it must look and sound authentic and none of this *Begorra* and *Bejaysus* stuff. Every so often Colin would squeeze my hand and say, 'Are you all right there Missus?' and I would be, then.

We booked into the Great Southern Hotel. Colin was booked in a single room, so he asked the porter for a double; he said his wife had come down with him. The man said, 'Oh yes, certainly sir, no trouble at all sir.' Colin signed 'Mr and Mrs Dempsey, Seapoint, Co. Dublin,' in the book.

We went up to our bedroom and he closed the door and pulled me against him and both of us fell onto the bed and we made love just like that, dressed. He had to rush out then to join the others and he was very excited and he said, 'It's almost like being a teenager, screwing like that, with your togs on,' and he gave me the name of the pub where they'd be doing the recording and said, 'Have a bath and a change and take a taxi down when you're ready.'

I nearly didn't go. I wanted to stay in the bedroom, to get into bed, to pull the sheets and blankets up, to keep it now, to keep it like now for ever.

Laughing sometimes you'd be frightened to stop and frightened to go on. A hand might come out of the sky and shout, 'Idiot!' and a huge thumb would squash you flat like a fly on the ground.

The next morning Colin said, 'You must come and live with me when we go back to Dublin.' I said, 'Yes, I will.'

He'd woken me up by making love to me and he said, 'I love you, come and live with me, you must come and live with me.' He was like that. He'd make it a very we-together situation if he liked you. I just thought, Yes, I'll go. I felt as if I'd been waiting a long time. Preparing.

We had breakfast in bed and we made love again and we had baths and we stood holding each other and I said, 'I'm frightened to go out into the world again.' And he held me tight against him and was saying, 'Poor scared dicky-bird, I'll protect you from the world.' And I believed him.

We moved my clothes and things into his flat the following week. It was out by the sea and you could hear that blue splashing sound day and night and the air was salty. Colin paid my landlord three weeks' rent in lieu of notice. I would have tried to creep out, or been terribly embarrassed; he'd just say, 'Okay what's the problem?' and solve it.

At the beginning we spent most of our time in bed. I was shy with him. With David it had been different. I felt I was the one with the power: the loved, not the lover. But now, now I was melting, and dissolving, and wondering.

Wondering about bodies. You couldn't believe their differences and their samenesses. A familiarity and then a yawning gulf of strangeness. Sometimes I lay back very still when we made love. I used to think of trying to avoid my stepmother's kisses when I was a child, of hating the English nun who was always trying to touch me. Yet here I was lying back allowing Colin make these fantastic intrusions into my body and into me. Sometimes one, sometimes both.

Sometimes you couldn't believe it, the things he would do with your body. There were times when he came in without touching, his face closed like a fist; you were completely separated and yet so stuck together, his eyes closed, your eyes open, him pulling and pulling until he finished and went to sleep—it was like a blind man trying to grasp something, desperately.

The first time he wanted me to kneel up and let him come in from behind I was saying, 'Ah no' and turning to him and he got very angry and said, 'Oh all right' and flung me back and thrusted himself in and in and threw himself off finally into a chasm of sleep and I lay awake, tears pouring down my face.

I remember saying, 'I love you' and wanting something more unique to say to him and Colin saying, 'Nobody's unique for Christ's sake.'

I'd feel terrified sometimes when we were together—nobody is allowed to feel so happy, so stretched into every corner of your skin that you'll burst. It can't last. Somebody will prick the edges.

I asked Colin one night whether he thought that for every high in life there had to be a low, for every smile a groan, a see-saw? I thought my voice sounded rather dramatic and silly but the question was serious.

He said, 'Is that what the nuns told you?' He laughed. I don't know, is that what they told us? But hasn't everyone else told us, ever since? The way they looked at us if we sang and held each other's arm and kissed suddenly in the middle of a grey, windy street? Haven't their eyes said it? *Oh you'll get what's coming to you*—their faces cocked, waiting for you to trip and fall. *One pays, and one pays, and one pays,* they would say.

Colin would say, 'Grab what you can. You've got a short breathing space between the helplessness of childhood and the hopelessness of old age. On either side there's a blank. Grab what you can, while you can.'

The best thing was going out together. Going to cinemas, to theatres, to restaurants. Holding on to him with the pavements creaming out for us and the houses friendly. At weekends we'd drive up to Glendalough with a bottle of wine and a picnic. We'd go and visit his friends who lived in a big old house in Enniskerry. They were a sort of commune. They all smoked pot and didn't take much notice of anyone new arriving. You felt rather silly and didn't know whether to sit or stand or what. You were starving and were scared to ask about food.

One night we met David and he was with a fat girl called Margaret who'd been in the year below me at school. She wore two sets of lipstick, one over the other; it made her lips look cracked, like an old painting. David looked at Colin with his crab's eyes and you almost expected him to go scuttling off sideways, back to his table. He had a tragic look on his face and you didn't even feel sorry for him. You were that arrogant in your love. Colin said he didn't understand how you could bear to go round with 'that lot'. I said, 'What lot?' He said, 'The get-rich-quick-boys from Foxrock.' I couldn't think of anything to say.

Colin was preparing a series of programmes on traditional singers and musicians all over Ireland. Sometimes he'd let me come with him. They'd be making films in old, dark pubs, and there'd be old men with eyes like rock pools, full of shadows, and young men with thick wrists sticking out of their jackets, and women, their eyes closed, listening to the weird winding tunes that were about the people's sorrows.

I'd sit and watch Colin working and think: How easily he does things. How sure he is. I'd never felt sure like that. I felt all my sureness from modelling had been just a fraud. It just showed you how to cover up, to make up, to fake up, and be something you weren't.

Colin had so many friends it was amazing. He said it was working in television; you met new people all the time. I'd think, Yes and you meet new girls all the time too, but wouldn't say it. That would be the kind of remark that would drive him mad. 'Yes, I like women,' he'd say, 'I love them.' He'd look at you with those black-brown eyes and then burst out laughing, and you'd laugh too.

He laughed when you told him about school. He'd say, 'Tell me the story of the night you pierced your ears again.' He said, 'For fuck's sake, those bloody nuns are terrible, the things they'd tell you.' He said Catholicism left you with a mark for life; you could never really enjoy yourself.

He'd gone to day school until he was fifteen and then his mother had died and his father had taken to drink and Colin had to leave school and look after him. He was earning ten pounds a week as copy boy in one of the newspapers; the basic was six pounds ten but he used to do overtime. His father drank most of the wages. Plus his pension. His father had a Republican pension from the Civil War, and another from the bank.

Colin's mother was the daughter of an English officer whose father had been stationed in Ireland. She was a very beautiful girl and all the men were after her. She met Colin's father when he had carried her brother home one night, dead drunk. She'd answered the door in her nightdress and helped carry the drunken brother upstairs. Her family said she was throwing herself away on a 'dirty little Republican' when she said she was going to marry him. They cut her off without a penny. She didn't mind.

They went on their honeymoon to Killarney.

When she was thirty-five she got multiple sclerosis. Bit by bit her body collapsed around her. It took five years. Colin said that she was like a vegetable in the end. He left home. He couldn't bear it. He said he'd have killed himself if he'd been the victim. I said, 'That's easy enough to say now.' He said, 'No. I mean it. I'd never inflict myself on people like that …' His voice was like a mangle—a grinding, choking voice. He almost hated her for staying alive.

One night he cried.

We'd been to a party. This friend of Colin's had been talking to me all evening. He was also working in television. He was very serious. He was a left-wing socialist, he said, and he talked about the class structure in Cork and I didn't really understand what he was saying but he had a lovely voice, like a cello's voice.

He said, 'I don't believe in going to bed with women unless I think I can convert them to socialism.' I thought that was very brave—stupid, but brave too. I pictured him in a night cap and striped nightshirt, holding a candle; sitting up all night, freezing on the edge of the bed talking about the Rights of Man.

Colin said, 'Bloody rubbish, he'll go to bed with anything in a skirt.' He said, 'What was old randy pants talking to you about anyway?'

I said, 'About classes in County Cork.'

Colin burst out laughing. I said, 'What are you laughing at?' We were sitting up in bed having a drink and a cigarette and talking about the party.

He said, 'And what would you know about the class structure in County Cork, may I ask?'

I said, 'Well there's nothing to stop me learning is there? Even if I didn't know before.'

We started arguing then and Colin said I was stupid, that I was pretentious. I didn't know what pretentious meant except from the way he said it: *Pretentious little whore.* I said, 'I'm not a whore.' He said, 'Well you got into bed with me quick enough, didn't you? Could hardly wait to get your little panties off, could you?'

He went on like that and I started crying and I was saying, 'I'm not a little whore,' and not knowing why not, and he was shouting, 'Well why spend the whole night flashing it at your left-wing socialist?'

Then I shouted at him, 'What, What, Whaaat?' and I couldn't believe he was jealous and he turned over and buried his head in the pillow and tears were sobbing out and he said, 'Love me, oh love me,' and I held on to him until he fell asleep.

I could feel a howling starting somewhere in a wilderness inside me. It was the mad man, the lunatic in the painting; the road rushing towards him and those elongated, tortured hands, holding the edges of his howling head together.

✺ 10 ✺

It was about six in the evening. It had been a dry, high-skied day. Colin had been at the studio since seven that morning, editing. He shouted through the letterbox for help to carry in some gear from the car.

I helped him in with the stuff: two new loudspeakers for the stereo and a box of records he'd bought at an auction. He started fiddling round with the equipment.

I thought: I won't say anything for a bit. I'll just be friendly and sweet. There's nothing men hate more than a naggy woman; women who pick on them for nothing. I'll pour him a drink, and myself another drink (a small one) and we'll sit down and talk about his day. Look at the sea. Decide what we'll do tonight. Perhaps we should go out somewhere for dinner. Relax. I'll ask him afterwards in bed. That will be best. When we're warm in bed. Now I'll just act completely normal, as if nothing has happened.

'Colin'—the words came bumping out, involuntarily—'where were you last night?' It had started. Too soon, too harsh, too sudden.

'Uh?' His back was turned to me and he was bending over the speakers, fitting them.

'I said, how did your meeting go last night? You must have

been quite late. I didn't hear you come in.' I'd heard. I'd lain awake in bed, stiff. He'd gone to sleep almost immediately. It was after one o'clock. He left for work at six-thirty that morning.

I got up and lit a cigarette. *Be calm, go easy, shut up. Colin will explain. He'll explain everything.*

Colin turned round and stood up. 'Now what the hell is the matter with you?' He walked towards me, put his hand out. 'You look as if you've seen a ghost.'

I laughed. A quick prism of a laugh, all angles and sharp lights. I turned and ran upstairs shouting in an uprush of tears, 'Bloody meeting indeed.'

I sat in front of the dressing table and looked in the mirror. Watching the tears streaking mascara rivulets down my cheeks. I thought of the nun telling us St Peter had two deep scars down his face from crying so much after he'd betrayed Jesus and got him crucified. The thing is once you start crying it's easier to start again the next time; you can go on indefinitely into madness, crossing deep streams of tears all the time, the world's tears.

Colin came in. He sat beside me on the stool and put his arm round me and then put his hand on my forehead. Like you would with a sick person. I took his hand in mine and bit it. It was bony, like biting a chicken's leg. I dropped it and screamed. He spun round. His hand felt flat; it cracked like India rubber against my face. He was shouting, 'You're hysterical' and going, *crack, crack*— across my face.

I was shouting through tears, 'Well why do you go out with little tarts and tell me you're at meetings? I saw you last night, I saw you going into the pub with a woman,' and saying it made it even worse; it was a turning, a twisting, a reality said and done, done first, then said.

Colin got up and said, 'If you're going to start prying on me, accusing me, then you can just piss off out of my life.' He was white-faced, his hands clenched. The words came out black and poisonous. Each one separately. Like sheep's shit.

'I'm not accusing, I'm not,' I said. 'I just want to know. I just don't understand what's going on, that's all.' I got up and took two steps towards him and he turned his back so I was just hold-ing his back and saying, 'Please, please, I'm sorry, I didn't want to make a scene, I've just been so miserable all day ...'

'I'm going out,' he said. He walked out of the room and down the stairs. He slammed the door. He slammed his car door. I could hear the engine right up the hill, the noise like a scar in the evening.

I lay down on the bed and cried until I was shaking all over. Until my face dissolved and my head expanded and I quaked. I gripped the pillow and when I stopped I'd torn it apart.

I got up and went into the bathroom. My face was red and purple and white. I made it smile at itself. It was a grotesque, frightened face with mad eyes. I bathed it. I mended it with pow-der and make-up and mascara. It was a clown's face, the pain bare under the layers of paint. It was a face that called out for annihi-lation. There was no way of doing it.

I went downstairs and poured another drink. And lit another cigarette. And thought, What do other people do in the same sit-uation? Nobody had ever been in the same situation. They would have told you.

I went over and over the scene. Oh, but I'd botched it. I'd acted like a damn dried-up wife. I'd accused, I'd cried, I'd screamed, I'd said, 'Where were you?' And Colin was free, he was a free man, I must never say, *Where were you?* as if I'd a right to know.

Jesus, I didn't mean to. I just wanted to know. I had a right to know hadn't I? *No. You can only know what he wants to tell.* Maybe he would have told—said, 'Oh I went out for a drink last night with the boss's wife while he was finishing the programme.'

Why? Am I not enough for him? Maybe I was not clever enough; I was always talking about clothes and things. Should I have been reading more? I thought, I should learn about television—talk to him about it.

I wished I'd never gone out with Valerie to that damn film. If I hadn't gone out I wouldn't have seen Colin with that girl. I wouldn't have known. It would have been better not to have known, not to know, wouldn't it? Or would it? Now, every time he went out I'd think he's with her. Every time he was out of the house I'd be squirming.

He'd probably been doing it for weeks. I was so blind with my idea of him I just wouldn't see. He's been sleeping with her probably as well. Rushing from home—a quick jab on the way to work. God, I could just see it.

Last night with Valerie I pretended it didn't matter. We'd gone on a schoolgirls' giggly outing for a change, without men; buses and peanuts, eyeing fellas in the interval. We were coming home, sitting on the upstairs section of the bus. We saw him walking arm in arm into the pub by the television station with this girl. Valerie said, 'Oh look, there's Colin,' and then looked at me, horrified. I'd looked out and laughed. I just saw their backs going in the door and I said, 'Oh he's a free man you know' and I hoped she'd think I was very sophisticated and blasé. Ah yes, Colin, my love. Colin with another … free … free to hate as much as he wanted and hurt as much as we were capable; that's what I was thinking by the following evening.

Damn him for doing it, oh God damn him. Why? We'd been so happy together. We were. We went everywhere together. Everyone said what a couple we were. All those nights I waited up for him in the gallery, watching him finish a show, thinking, That's Colin, he's mine, I love him.

I gave up the job in the library at College so I could be with Colin the mornings he was off work. We made breakfast and then made love afterwards and went into town. I hadn't even done modelling for weeks now. He never said anything much but I could see he didn't like me spending all that time with photographers, and pictures in magazines and stuff; he said it was like having a share in a bit of public property.

I didn't mind not working, not modelling. I wanted to live for Colin. I used to say to him, 'I'll die for you Colin.' He'd laugh and say, 'Much better to live for me Liz—what would I do with a beautiful corpse?'

What would I do? I had no money now. No flat. Nothing. I couldn't go home—they'd never really wanted me there. I couldn't just run in and say *Look after me*. They'd laugh, or be puzzled.

Please Colin come back, please. I'll do anything you want, anything. You can go out every night with anyone you like. I'll swear I'll never ask questions again. I'll just be here, waiting. Please, please.

The doorbell rang. Valerie. 'My God—what's the matter? You look in a right bloody mess.' I clutched at her. 'Oh Val, Colin's gone.' Saying it, shouting it, convincing myself, an echo: gone, *gone, gone.*

Valerie poured drinks and lit cigarettes. 'Ballast for disaster,' she said. She said, 'You're a right bloody fool. It's he who should be crying, not you. Get a grip on yourself. Damn men, they're all the same, want their cake and eat it, and want to be approved of for doing it as well. Give him a good kick if I were you. You can't let people use you like that.'

I kept saying, 'Oh but I want him back.' I was defending Colin. Valerie was saying, 'Ye gods and little fishes, he'll come back won't he? This is his flat isn't it? He's not going to abandon all his stuff for a start now is he?' Valerie talked on. She talked with the conviction someone has when analyzing somebody else's problem.

She said, 'The thing with men is never to show that you care. Oh you can be nice to them, and have a good time with them, but go mooney-eyed at them and you've had it. Kaput.'

Valerie said she had three fellas on the hook, different nights, different moods, different men. She said, 'It's time women started getting their own back a bit.' I said, 'I bit him on the hand.' We both laughed a bit crazily.

At midnight Valerie had to go to meet one of the three fellas. She said, 'For pity's sake Liz, don't let him get you down.' She made a face and squeezed my arm. 'Don't let him rule your bloody life.'

After she'd gone I walked round the living room for a bit. I opened the windows that looked out over the sea. I turned off the lights. The tide was coming in. Thousands of silvered ghosts chatting towards the shore, shifting and circling and hesitating but always moving forward. The air was thick with the smell of seaweed, a brown-yellow smell that slipped past your head and into the room, pushing into every corner. I thought, I'll just be sitting here calmly when Colin comes back. I'll say, 'Oh hello there,' as if nothing had happened. Bleakly I decided: Valerie's right, I mustn't let him rule my life.

I waited an hour. Another hour. The whiskey didn't seem to be having any effect—on me who got drunk on two glasses of wine! I thought, I can move around, I could hold a perfectly lucid conversation. I've got this slice round the top of my head which is crystal clear.

Where is Colin?

The hours gathered up like humps once they were over. Like black rocks. The minutes that made them up were mocking dancers, stretching and twanging sharp shut like elastic bands.

If I went out for a walk down to the sea then he may have come back and wondered where I'd gone. He may have gone off again. He may have thought I'd left. *I must stay.* The furniture was mocking me. The house was. Everything was. The moon was white with the joke of the whole thing. Why me? Why?

I felt my jeans being dragged off. It was Colin. I'd fallen asleep on the sofa. He was pulling at my clothes. His breath was thick with smells. He was saying, 'Fucking clothes' and trying to pull them off. I half sat up and pulled the rest of them off and I got down on the floor and wrapped the rug round the two of us and we made love like animals, sucking at each other as if we'd die of thirst.

∾ II ∾

'All I said was, "I think I'd like to go to College," or do something, anyway.'

'You're crazy Liz, what the hell do you want to go to College for?'

We were sitting up in bed; at least I was sitting up. Colin was lying down. It was eleven o'clock in the morning. I'd been thinking about the College business for days. College, somewhere to go every day. The books I'd read, the people I'd meet, the thoughts I'd have. Something.

'Isn't my baby happy here?' Colin put his head on my stomach. 'Isn't my Lizzie happy with her man?' He started stroking my legs and rubbing his head up and down on my belly.

I put my hand on his head. I said, 'Of course I'm happy. I just thought, well, I'm not sure, but I thought … Colin wait a minute… I thought …'

∽ 12 ∽

'We'll go to Paris for a holiday. How would you like that Liz?' We were sitting up again. 'You're just bored with Dublin I think. I've got to go to a film festival in France in four weeks' time. We'll meet up in Paris on the way back and have a holiday—d'ya like that Liz?'

I said, 'Yes. I'd like that.' I meant it too. But I also felt something had gone wrong. I'd given in too easily. It was always like that.

Maybe when we came back from Paris we would be able to talk about the College thing again. Colin was probably right anyway: I just needed a break. I'd never have the discipline to go to College, I supposed. I was too stupid as well. I mean, half the books that Colin had here were double Dutch to me: *Iron in the Soul* by Jean Paul Sartre—I tried reading it once but it was just words which seemed as though they'd been thrown at the page.

I couldn't make them string together.

That thing with the girl had been a shock too. For a week we'd been strangers to each other. Locked in the flat, viciousness of suspicion, watching each other.

Then we began to talk again. Snows freeze over green fields and black streams gush below. Everything looks like a blanket of white but underneath it's growing, and seething, and hot.

Colin said that he loved me, but that he must always feel free to have affairs with other women besides me. Not, he said, that he was having, or planning, an affair with that girl. No, that was just a friendly drink. He was calm. He made crying and hysteria and shouting seem ludicrous.

He said, 'I'm not blackmailing you, or bargaining with you,

but if you want to stay then you'll have to give me freedom to move as I want to, that is all.' Perhaps I said yes too readily. He said I should go out more.

The day after we'd talked about me going to College I dropped Colin at the television studios and took the car on into town. He'd given me a cheque for fifty pounds. He said, 'Get a facial or whatever you call it, and something new to wear.'

I went along to Suzanna's. She said, 'Long time no see,' and, 'When are you going to do some more work?' and 'You're not *married* or anything are you?' She kept up questions like that all the time she was cleaning and patting and toning. And although she only half expected an answer she was listening all the time too.

I rang David from Suzanna's office. Colin was going to be working all day. I thought, David will cheer me up. Anyway, David's an old friend. Colin knows him. It's all quite straightforward.

'You're looking beautiful,' David said, 'I've missed you.'

'Oh come on now,' I laughed, 'Don't look sad, you're supposed to be cheering me up, remember?'

David was pleased too. The other men in the bar were looking at us. At me. Sideways looks over their glasses, through their conversations, pretending not to really look at all, but wondering what it would take to lay you, peeling you off layer by layer, and barking at their wives when they got home.

We had drinks first. Campari cocktails. David hailed a couple of friends. He talked about his work. He kept saying, 'How *are* you?' but he really meant, 'How am I? Ask me, how am I?'

We went to this fish restaurant for lunch. It was a beautiful restaurant. There were white linen tablecloths that came down to the ground and then shorter, smaller, yellow linen squares that just covered the tabletops. There were heavy silver fish knives which slipped into the golden soft fish like a thieves. The waiters were dignified guardians of heaven. Slowly, slowly, they introduced you to all the delights that they were in charge of. 'A little more wine Madam? Perhaps a lightly tossed salad? Some cheese maybe? And a cigar for the gentleman … yes.'

They were mostly men who ate in this restaurant. In suits. Expensive suits. They were all very quiet. Nobody got rowdy or drunk or clicked their fingers at the waiters. Even David's lot were quiet if they come here. They came humbly, to worship.

'What would you do if I jumped on the bar and stripped?' I looked at David, laughing, the wine like white glass in my head. 'Oh Elizabeth,' David said.

I thought, I'll do it. I'll give them all a good fright. I'll strip and then walk out into the street, starkers—that will give them something to think about. I thought, Something, anything ... I was in that sort of mood. The world smothering me.

'What are you thinking about?' David gave my hand a squeeze. His was moist.

'I'm thinking how horrible I was to you. I used you,' I said. I thought: Did I though? Didn't he use me too? Taking me round because I looked like the right shape, and the right size, and didn't do anything too out of the ordinary?

'You could pay me back a little,' David said, squeezing my hand again. 'You could stay with me for the afternoon. We'll go and take a room in the Shelbourne.' He rushed the words. You could see it was the first time he'd dared proposition a woman like that.

We didn't say anything for a bit. His hand was sitting over mine on the table. The waiter smiled—thought we were lovers. I thought, Okay, I'll go with him to the Shelbourne. I'll go like a proper tart.

A hotel room in the middle of the afternoon—Jesus!

The man at the reception desk had a face like a wasp, bunched-forward eyes and eyebrows and nose all in one. He said, 'Mr and Mrs ...?' and paused. I wished I hadn't come. 'Luggage, sir?', and he paused. This man dropped in a pause each time he asked a question—*Fill that if you can, you clowns.*

The room was right at the end of this carpeted passage. The carpet was so thick; you felt as though you had cotton wool in your ears. Sounds were different. Muffled.

David picked up the phone and rang for two double whiskies. 'No, better make it a bottle of whiskey, Jameson, and some water.' I looked out the window onto the street below. There were all these people in their coats and trousers and dresses shopping and going home, eating the food and wearing out the clothes and then coming back and shopping again. The closed circles of our lives. I thought, I'll open the window and scream, I'll say, 'Drop your shopping, lift up your skirts and live.' I imagined their little saucer faces turning up. Shock. Surprise. I thought, I'll have to do something. This is awful.

David came over. He put his arms round me, crossed across my front, a hand round each breast. He put his nose in my hair, snuffling. 'Oh baby, my baby.'

There was a knock at the door. The waiter: 'Excuse me sir, your whiskey.' Your room, your whiskey, your tart, your money … *Sir.*

The waiter left. I said, looking in my bag for a cigarette, 'Look David, I'm sorry, but I can't really go to bed with you. I mean it wouldn't be fair on Colin. Or you.' David winced at that last bit. He handed me a whiskey. 'Have a little drink anyway.' His face was crumpled-looking. A foetus face. We had two large whiskies. I turned on the radio above the bed. It was Johnny Cash. 'I find it very, very easy to be true; I find myself alone when each day's through; Yes I'll admit that I'm a fool for you; Because you're mine I'll toe the line …' Something like that. I began humming to it. We used to sing it at school and long for someone to be a fool for, somebody to toe the line for.

The whiskey was changing the room, making it warmer. The corners were softening. The bed stopped looking like a coffin. David was sitting in the chair with a smile on his face, his hand circling my ankle; I was rocking in time to the music, sitting on the bed … la la da dee da.

'I'll give you three hundred pounds it you will sleep with me.' David's voice was absurd. His eyes were small. His face pinched. He pulled out his cheque book and made out the cheque. I thought, This isn't happening. It's a joke. David is joking. We're just having a little drink and talking about some things.

'Will you?' His face was red, pleading. I thought, David you mustn't plead like that. I wanted to tell him. It made me feel awful. I thought, Okay, I'll do it. If he wants it so badly then I'll do it. It was almost as if my body didn't belong to me. I sometimes felt that.

We got out of our clothes, hurriedly, David trembling. I started shivering all over. The sheets were so cold. So clean. We covered our bodies with the sheets. David was saying, 'Oh Liz'—and I felt so cold. I thought: *I'm the moon. I'm one eye, one silver eye, that's as cold as metal.* I concentrated on keeping my head up, straight. I thought, If I don't move, if my head doesn't look at what's going on down there it will be as if it hasn't happened.

David rolled off. Dry. Exhausted. I felt a surge of pity for him. Sorry. I felt disgust. I thought I want to get out of there, quick. I wanted the flat, the sea, Colin. I was putting on my clothes, rubbing between my legs with this scratchy white towel with 'Hotel Shelbourne' printed on it in flowery writing. I turned round to him before I left. I put my hand on his head. I said, 'I'm sorry David, so sorry' and then ran out, down the corridor, down the stairs, across the hallway—the man at the desk said in his wasp's voice, 'Anything wrong Madam?' 'Piss off,' I shouted, running out. I thought, For Christ's sake, what's the *matter* with me?

∽ 13 ∽

I drove from the hotel out to home. Family home, not our flat (Colin's flat really).

I was thinking of something I'd read in a magazine about murderers always returning to the scene of their crime and I was wondering whether that was why I wanted to go back and abase myself in front of David, and whether that was why I wanted to go home. I was thinking, Does everyone feel this sense of having committed a crime? Not all the time, but having sometimes a very strong sense of guilt, an awareness of at some stage being, perhaps billions of years ago, party to something horrible. It remains as a little deformity inside you.

I was thinking about Father and about Mary. I thought, 'They never touched me very much as a child.' I was surprised at that.

I'd never thought of it before. Suddenly I could feel the lack of their hands around me.

There was another article I read in the same magazine that talked about murderers. This one talked about people's spines shrivelling if they are *not touched* enough. They used the word *touch* to mean both physical and spiritual touching. They said that every human being needs a certain amount of touching to remain healthy; it is as vital as food, they said. You could touch somebody emotionally, according to this article, by just saying 'Good morning' to them in a friendly sort of way, or you could make their spine shrivel by ignoring their smile at a bus stop. An amazing article.

Father opened the door. He said, 'My Lizzie! You're a woman already.' He stood still with his hand on the door, looking at me. I said, 'A surprise visit—and a flying one—from your prodigal daughter.' I kissed him on the cheek.

Mary heard the voices from the kitchen. She came out, her hands covered in flour. She must have been baking bread. She walked up and we stood in the hall.

She lifted her hands to show me the flour and that she couldn't hug me and she smiled; there was a tiny silence, like a gasp; then we all said something together.

Mary said, 'Come into the living room. We're just going to have tea.' She was shy. Almost as if I were a stranger. I was a stranger. She said, 'Mmm very smart,' and made me turn around so she could see my dress, but she wasn't sure about it. It was a smock. You could see she thought they were just for pregnant women.

Mary brought in tea. The cherry tree in the garden had silken branches of deep ochre. The windows were open onto the garden. The *zing* of the cars from the main road and the garden smells came through.

We talked about events. Occurrences. About Father's book which was with the publishers. About the flu Mary had had. About the people who'd moved in next door. Father looked a lot older than a month before when I'd seen him in town. I hadn't been to this house for seven months. Quite a feat, given the nearness of it. But then distances are always to do with love, or lack of it, seldom with space.

Father wanted to know why I gave up the job in College: 'I thought you liked it so much?'

I said, 'I get plenty of money from modelling you know. You can earn up to one hundred pounds for just one session.' They didn't like that. You could see they were thinking: that kind of money just means badness. At least Mary was thinking that—to Father it was probably meaningless.

'I'm going to Paris for a week,' I said. 'For a holiday.'

Mary smiled. 'Oh that will be nice for you.' She said it flatly. Modelling and Paris and one hundred pounds—what would she tell her friends when they asked, 'And how's our Elizabeth doing these days?'—the competition for your kids' careers—*Is my one better than yours?*—and all hidden under smiles of concern and interest.

'I'm going with a group of friends,' I said. 'Some people from the television station.' That would be something to tell them—wouldn't it?

I told them I'd moved flats, that I was sharing with a girl-friend who had a flat out by the sea. I said we lived with the sound of the sea in our heads, day and night.

I wanted to say clever things. To say: 'Look, I'm okay, and I made it, and who would have thought it?' Things like that. I wanted to say sad things as well: 'Why didn't you touch me more when I was a child? Why did you never love me?'

I wanted to say, 'You've changed and I've changed, and we've changed in spite of each other, but we could still perhaps learn to know, even to like.'

I wanted to say, 'I'm living with Colin, the young man who was making the film about the history of Ireland. I'm a grown-up woman now, I'm not a virgin any more, I don't go to Mass any more, I even sleep with men in the middle of the afternoon, and for money, and last week I got so drunk I conked out.'

I wanted to say, 'Tell me what you're most afraid of. Tell me your very favourite thing in the whole world.' I wanted to try to tell them why I didn't, couldn't, come round more often ... all sorts of things. It was too late or too early.

We talked about the weather. We talked about the price of

food and how everything was going up these days. Father talked about the state of the country and Mary said, 'I don't know what the world is coming to.' We were very solemn, each in a chintz chair, slapping phrases like plasters over each other's words, or wounds, the one hiding the other.

I excused myself and went upstairs to the bathroom. The house looked so small—a doll's house. I went into my bedroom and lay down on the bed. Mary had left my room as if I was about to come back from school for the long holidays, or home from a trip abroad. There were posters of pop stars with marble eyes and shiny, every-day-washed hair and pink lips; there was another poster on 'Exercising your way to Beauty' and a course for twenty-eight weeks; there were two dolls sitting on the mantelpiece, their plastic legs stuck straight out in front of them, their blue-flecked eyes unwinking.

I thought, You change and you change and you change, but all the time you carry the corpse of your younger self inside you. Your body gets bigger and fuller and riper, then smaller and thinner and drier, yet all the time there's yourself and the thrust of what you really wanted to be, buried inside you.

I went into the bathroom. Automatically I started making up my face. A bit of powder, a bit of mascara.

Something fell out of my bag onto the floor. I picked it up. It was David's cheque. He must have stuffed it into the bag before I left. I suddenly wanted to laugh. How would I have explained that one to Colin? *Oh just a little gift from an old admirer, darling.*

It was one of those days when each event cancels out the one that went before. You live without responsibility. You feel a little melancholy, but it's a friendly melancholy. You can afford to laugh at your own ludicrousness.

I crumpled the cheque up into a ball and flushed it down the loo. The water tank coughed and sneezed and shook its shoulders and then righted itself and then quietened down to refilling. A busy, soothing sound. The cheque came bobbing up again in the bowl. Buoyant, Bank of Ireland paper.

I fished the cheque out and wrapped it in some toilet paper

and put it into the special zipper pocket inside the lining of my bag. When I'd bought the bag it carried a tag advertising the zipper pocket as 'A secret pouch for the Mysterious Lady'. I'd never used it before. I thought, I'll burn the cheque when I get back to the flat.

I told Mary and my father that I had to go. I said I was being taken out to dinner by that young man who was making a film about the history of Ireland. I wanted them to hear his name again, to be reminded of him, to know of his link with me. We said goodbye at the door. I said that Mary must come and have lunch with me one day, in town. I was into the car, and waving, and starting the engine, and then gone.

I belted the car down the road. I thought, I'm a balloon. If anything hits me it will just bounce off. I thought, It's only four o'clock in the afternoon and I'm a changed person since this morning. I've had my face changed, and my body changed, and my childhood changed.

I sang in the car. I sang Johnny Cash. I felt my body. Every edge and surface of it. I felt how it touched the air. I thought of it replacing a body of air, like Archimedes getting into his bath and replacing a body shape of water. It was about the only piece of our science course I could remember.

Colin said I was stupid. I didn't think I was. I felt things. I thought, If you were stupid you wouldn't feel things—or not very much. I thought that once you felt things then the rest was just going to college or something like that.

Colin and his friends talked about things the whole time. They sat around pouring thick brown gravy of talk into each other. For hours. I liked listening to them. Sometimes I felt like saying, 'Colin, couldn't we just go to bed now?' But I knew Colin would kill me if I said that. I once said I couldn't understand Jean Paul Sartre; that it was all just words. Colin looked at me. They all stopped talking. Colin said, 'For God's sake, Elizabeth.' He said it like a curse.

Colin was very good to me though. Giving me that cheque this morning for instance. *Cheque,* I thought, *cheque.* Poor David and his damn cheque. I hoped he'd left the hotel by now. It seemed like years ago. Imagine pleading like that. *Will you do it for three hundred pounds?*

I couldn't imagine Colin pleading. He wasn't that sort of person. At work he really shouted at the men in the studio but they didn't seem to mind. They all went down to the pub later and drank. Colin liked really rough pubs. He said, 'That's where the Real People are.' He said I was a terrible snob, but I just didn't know what to say to those people.

Another thing he did was to read comics. He and these two friends, they'd rush down to the newsagent on Fridays to get their comics: 'Dangerman!' and 'Batman!' and they lined up with the poor kids and they bought about six comics each and the kids just bought one. They had their money ready in pennies and halfpennies. Colin and his friends paid with pounds.

Colin said, 'Comics are part of our culture; they're indicative.' I thought they were just for kids. I thought culture meant art galleries and Tolstoy and things like that—heavy, polished, difficult things.

Colin could be difficult. He could be hard. His eyes could go like diamonds. His face would shut down. He'd go on like that if his father came round. His father lived in a room in Blessington Street. He came round to beg money and maybe he just wanted to be talked to as well. Once he wept and held on to Colin's knees. I've sometimes sat for a whole morning, giving him coffee and cigarettes, while he was shaking and dribbling and waiting for Colin to come. Colin said I shouldn't let him in. But he cries through the letterbox.

Colin said, 'I'm not his bloody nursemaid. If the old bastard wants to drink himself to death then let him.' I thought, That's an awful thing to say about your own father. Colin said, 'And a lot you know about it dear.'

Colin drank a lot too. Not when he was working; he'd never drink when he's working. But at night. Sometimes he'd get so drunk it was frightening. He'd become a different person. Cruel. He wouldn't let me talk about it afterwards. Once he said, 'Like father, like son.' He threw a chair through the window and was shouting and I burst into tears. He was like a mad person. He punched me in the face; he said, 'Shut up your bloody cater-wauling.' I had to tell people I'd fallen down the steps. They all smiled: *Tsch, tsch.* They knew.

I'd come to the railway crossing. It was 4.30 p.m. I thought, I'll cross the railway. I'll go and sit on the sand for a little bit.

The sea was grey. It was like a whale. Wet, solid and grey. Every so often it shifted. The sand was wettish. The grains stuck like wet salt when you tried to let them run through your fingers. The sun had sort of diluted itself throughout the sky. The sun leaked a pale yellow into the whole, sodden sky.

I thought, I'm hardly ever on my own. I was often alone in the flat in the sense that there wasn't another person around: Colin had gone to work and I was there alone, but I put on records very loud, I did my exercises, I gave myself home facials, or hair conditioners, or I cooked something for our lunch. I never stopped. I never sat down and said, 'Now, just think.'

I picked up this book once in the house of one of Colin's friends. It said (or said something like) this: 'Think of a grey wall. Think of a completely grey wall covering your mind. Think of all your thoughts imprisoned behind that wall, unable to get out. Look at the wall in your mind. Let yourself be blank, blank. Then slowly watch as thoughts present themselves to you.' This was to do with relaxation or something. The book was to exercise the mind in ways of thought.

I sat looking at the sea. I thought, That's my grey wall. I tried to think blank, blank. Did the wall have bricks? No. My hair tickled my face. The sand was cold. I thought: I'll walk along and think of a blank wall.

I thought of Colin and me. Always. I was always thinking of Colin and me. Is it love? I don't know. People say it's love when you think of the other person the whole time.

I thought, This is me. This is Elizabeth O'Sullivan, walking along Sandymount Strand. I thought: I'm twenty. I thought: People die when they're twenty. The following year they vote. They can be hanged when they're eighteen. They can get married when they're sixteen. In England the upper classes send their boys to boarding school when they're eight. They put their names down for public schools the day after they're born.

All those different ages.

I thought: I'm twenty and I've done nothing. I thought, That's very melodramatic. I'm three years away from school. All those years and I've done nothing. I thought, *Who am I?* Twenty, and I'm nothing. But I have Colin, haven't I? If Colin decides he likes that girl with the long hair in the pub—what am I then?

Valerie said there are plenty more where they come from. Meaning men. I thought of Valerie in big Wellington boots, fishing in the Atlantic with a huge fishing rod, for men.

I thought: Well if Colin leaves there's always David. I could go to David and throw myself on his mercy. I could say, 'David, David, forgive me. I've been so awful, so unfaithful, such a harlot, forgive me David.'

I could get married to David. Everybody gets married. Eventually. Colin said, 'Why the hell get married? Particularly in Ireland.' David and I could be married and live in a house. We'd give dinner parties. I'd shop in town. I'd probably have a lover. It might be Colin. Everybody in Foxrock had lovers. So.

I thought: You're tired. You need a holiday. Colin is right. All you need is a rest. You're twenty and you've got what you wanted, right? You've got Colin, you've got your flat together, well his flat, but you're living there; you've got everything.

Haven't you?

You felt scared. Scared he'd leave you? He ruined everything by going out with that girl; but that's stupid. All these men have affairs. Anyway he said it was nothing. He said, 'I suppose it's all right if I have a drink with a friend?' He said it in this very sarcastic voice. You said, 'Yes of course, it's just …' 'Just what?' he said. You said, 'Oh nothing.'

You went to bed with people, like David. Why? You lived with Colin, you felt you needed his reassurance. You wanted him saying, *Yes,* and *No,* and *I like that,* or *I don't.* You knew what it was like to be on your own. Even if Colin was angry or cross at least he was there. He'd take you round, show you things, laugh with you. A hand to stretch out to in the middle of the night. Someone to smile at during the ghastly party. A person to write letters to: foolish, intimate things.

I thought about going to bed with people and how that had changed, coming from school where I'd lived with the nuns' puritanism and the threat and danger of sex; and then sleeping with people and finding the heavens didn't fall on you, like the nuns said, or open up for you, like the magazines said. Sometimes it worked, sometimes it didn't. There was nothing magical. Growing up, I read somewhere, is when you stop having recourse to moods and masturbation.

But you were young still, weren't you? No need to worry. No need to worry about your life, you'd lots of time yet to think about it — to think about what you were going to do. Anyway lots of women didn't have jobs, or careers, or anything. Why should you? Colin said, 'It's *petit bourgeois* conformism to want a job.' He said, 'Are you scared of living your life from minute to minute? Of not having schedules, timetables, targets?'

I was sure Colin was right. You just needed a rest. Still you thought, What's the matter with me?

∽ **14** ∽

'Do you want to go to the party, or not?'

'Oh, I don't know.'

'*Do* you?'

'Couldn't we just stay in and be together on our own for a change, just for once?'

'We've been asked to go. A few minutes ago you were madly enthusiastic.'

'It's just … I don't know … it's just we never seem to talk to each other at parties. I don't quite know how to put it . . .'

'You don't go to parties to talk to each other, stupid. You go to meet people.'

'Oh yes, we all know why you go to parties — to meet girls.'

'So we're back on that one again. You're becoming like a bloody, nagging wife, Elizabeth.'

'Darling, I'm sorry. I didn't mean to be awful, it's just . . .'

'Look. All I want to know is whether you want to go to the fucking party or not, uh?'

'Yes. Yes, I'll come to the party.'

∽ 15 ∽

I still think, that damned party.

It began with the argument: would we go, or wouldn't we. Colin said he had been stuck all day in the bloody editing room and now he wanted some fun. I wanted to stay in and talk to him. So many things happen and you fear you'll lose them by to-morrow, feelings, tentative feelings. Then I said the thing about him wanting to go just to meet girls. There are times when you want peace and you want to sit at home in old jeans and watch television, or at least that's what you think might help. *Something.* I get tired of the battles outside. Colin said, 'You want us to end up arthritic and snivelling over a coal fire, locked into endless, old-age boredom.' The kind of thing you couldn't answer.

I started getting dressed. Colin came up and watched me. He was very fussy about my clothes. He came shopping with me; he said, 'Well seeing that you dress for the delectation of men, they should be the best judges of what looks good on you.' I used to like it when he came shopping.

Now he was in one of those moods. Drinking. A bottle of whiskey in one hand, he lay on the bed and talked about work, and how those 'fucking morons of production assistants could never read a studio script right, even if you shoved it under their bloody noses.' You'd have to watch him. He might easily hurt you—a sort of Catherine wheel spinning off thousands of sparks: the fairy princess might get burnt up.

He was laughing and telling me about a girl he went to bed with once who had false teeth. He couldn't get an erection, seeing this girl with her lips napping together like a fish's and re-membering the teeth quietly floating in milky liquid in the bathroom. Completely de-sexed him. She'd got a disease of the gums when she was a kid and her teeth had all fallen out.

She'd said she took them out because some people found it more disconcerting if they heard a clicking noise halfway through. The clicking false teeth make when you're eating or doing something strenuous, she said.

I went to bed once with this friend of Colin's with smelly teeth; you'd have thought it would have been his breath that smelt but his teeth were so yellow and ancient, I'm sure it must have been them. His name was John; he was a poet or something. Everyone said he was very good. It was at a party and Colin had been talking to a girl for hours and John was rolling joints and giving me the eye, and I'd thought, What the hell, anything goes.

It was pretty sordid really. Colin was chatting up this girl, and then John said, 'Oh come on,' and 'Don't be such a frigid Brigid.' I started watching for Colin and hoping he'd come out and then I'd smile at John and pretend to be listening to him, and Colin could damn well see that I was fine without him, but eventually John and I ended up in a bedroom upstairs on a pile of coats and anoraks. He didn't take off his clothes and I just closed my eyes against the smell of his teeth. Colin had never even noticed that I'd left the room.

I was thinking, The thing is, you can never trust women. A man has just got to smile at them and they're falling over him. I mean, Colin was one of those men that liked women. He liked the whole business of sex and flirting and stuff. You could see the women responding. Some of them envied you and said, 'You're lucky.' In a way you thought you were—such a good, sexy catch. Nobody wanted a guy that nobody else was going to fancy; there'd have to be something wrong with him. But then you knew yourself, easy come and easy go, and that's how you were, into bed the first night he asked you, and if everyone else was like that there was nothing to prevent him, was there?

A woman would never think like that about a man. She'd never say: Oh he's a good type, or a bad type, depending on how long the gap between the time they met and the time they went to bed together. A woman would think: This is a special man, who is making this very special and exclusive gesture towards me. She wouldn't be able to bear it if she thought the man could just as easily have screwed the little dark girl over in the corner.

Colin was saying, 'There's a girl I want you to meet tonight, she's called Mary.'

I'd always hated that name. *Mary.* It was weighted with religion and stupidity and prejudices. My stepmother's name.

Colin said, 'She's Ruth's latest *protégée*—disarmingly honest.' I wanted to go to the party even less.

Ruth was a lady producer in television. It was she who was giving the party. She produced 'special' programmes. Heavies. She and Colin had an affair about two years ago which was how he'd become a director. He'd been designing the studio sets for a programme Ruth was producing and they'd started sleeping together. Ruth thought Colin's mind was wasted on graphic design work. She got him onto this directors' course. Colin said they were always more interested in each other's minds than each other's bodies. I said, *Mmm.* We used to laugh about him sleeping his way to the top in television, just like a starlet in Hollywood or a secretary in the BBC.

All the time I was dressing, I had a feeling about this party — that something awful was going to happen. Something. I wanted to kiss Colin, to say, 'You'll never hurt me, will you?', and couldn't, and knew that he would, some day.

The party was the beginning of the end, or the other way round, depending on how you remembered it.

So it was at this party that I first met Mary. I was with Angus, a friend of Colin's, who was married to a girl called Miriam and they both slept with everyone and anyone. Angus and I were talking to each other and pretending to be interested and interesting, and Ruth had taken Colin off to meet some Italian journalist who was preparing a script for a film on the 'Death of Dublin'.

A girl came up and said, 'Hello, I'm Mary. Colin has told me about you.' (I hate it when people say that.) She wore old blue jeans and a t-shirt. She spoke straight out, like a man, and shook hands. She said she'd just come back from two years in France where she'd started off selling copies of the *New York Herald Trib-*

une and ended up singing in cafés, and in France, she said, everyone shakes hands the whole time.

Angus, randy Angus, was widening his eyes at her and she wasn't even bothering. She was talking to me, and I was looking round for a man to latch on to. She was asking me what I did and I said, 'I just *am*.' Men usually thought that interesting, to just *be*, ('so delightfully unplebeian,' as Angus would say). She just gave this odd look.

I said, 'Colin says it's simply *petit bourgeois* conformism to want to work.' She burst out laughing, and said, 'God, some men are incredible.' I wasn't sure what she meant but I didn't like her, and her damned open-ended laugh.

We talked about various things and then Angus asked me to dance and he put his hand on my bottom and I cuddled up to him and both of us knew it would come to nothing. Then the Italian journalist came over and said he'd like to use me in his film, and Colin and I were to have dinner with him the following night.

The Italian was all smouldering eyes and tight Italian shirt and trousers and knowing, sexy looks. He and Mary started talking about Dublin—Mary had been brought up in the Coombe by a grandmother and that is one of the oldest parts of Dublin left so she promised to take this Italian around.

I looked round but couldn't see Colin. I presumed he'd gone to the loo or something. The Italian journalist took a bottle of whiskey out from under his jacket and I went off to the kitchen to get cups and some water.

Ruth's house was a bungalow. It looked out over Bray. She bought it cheap from an American playwright who had it specially designed for himself and was going to live in it, and write, and be inspired by Ireland; he only lasted a month and went off shouting it was the 'most Goddawful country in the world', and, 'the women—Jesus H. Christ!'

All the rooms in the house opened into each other. The kitchen was in the centre of the house with the guest room off one end and the living room off the other. This was to allow guests to fix themselves drinks or food or whatever without tramping through the family's area. The door to the guest room was slightly open. The light was off. There was some sort of noise, somebody in there. I listened for a minute and then realized there were two people in there. The bed was creaking and I could hear a girl going, Ooh, mmm, ahh—the private moans of love. Odd to hear them; usually you make them yourself so you don't think of them as existing separately from the physical feeling of making love. I walked over to close the door feeling knowing, indulgent.

The light from the kitchen made a narrow yellow path into the room. I could make out two figures thrashing on the bed.

I stopped dead.

My hand was on the door handle. Black hands coming over my face, my eyes, my consciousness, spinning … spinning …

It was Colin on the bed. Colin and some woman.

I closed the door. Turned round. Went back to the sink. Gripping the cold steel sink, the cold wet hard feeling drove into my bones, like a kid in a comic who's just been hit on the head with a mallet, the spinning stars and bolts, and then turning and out of the kitchen door and scrabbling among a pile for my coat, and the car keys, and keeping my back to the people in the other room—thinking like a child, If I don't look, they won't see me. Then my whole body turning electric, my head transparent, and thinking, If anyone touches me I'll disintegrate, dissolve; and picking up the coat and saying to myself, Be calm, be white calm, but go, go quickly before the disintegration. Don't scream, don't make a fuss, just go; soon they'll all be laughing at you, soon, but not now, don't wait, get out before their faces follow you, laughing, laughing, laughing …

I was running down the road to the car. It was like those awful dreams when your heart pounds and you run and run and run but your legs have turned to liquid plastic and they *squodge* onto the pavements and stick and your arms are outstretched and something awful is following you and you know you'll never make it round the corner.

I heard footsteps following. I got to the car. Tried to get the keys in. Stuffing them in. Which are the bloody, bloody keys, oh God help me find the keys and then—

A hand on my shoulder. I turn round. It was Mary.

'What's happened to you?' she was saying. 'I saw you charging out the door. What's the matter?' and I was screaming, 'Just go away and leave me alone—everyone go away.' There wasn't anyone else. Just Mary.

I was shouting and crying and thinking I must go, now, now, NOW.

Mary was saying, 'Wait a minute, you can't drive a car in that condition,' and then she was holding me and I had my head down on her shoulder and tears were pouring out and she was just holding and saying 'Okay now, okay,' and I was wanting to drain my whole self out through my eyes, a hot liquid, let it pour and pour and then I'd no longer be, I'd just be a flowing stream, and Mary just held on to me and gradually I began to ease down again.

I pulled up straight. Sniffing, wiping my face. All I could think of again was running, going.

'Have a cigarette,' Mary said and pulled out a packet and lit one for herself and held up the light to me and my hands were shaking so much I could hardly hold the cigarette. She didn't look at me. We stood there in the moonlight, smoking, and then she said, 'Walk a little bit. It's often better if you walk.' So we started walking up the road and then I could feel the pain creeping back again and the tears coming up and this terrible confusion in my head and had to stop and I couldn't remember what I was saying except something like 'Help me, help me,' and I was holding on to her.

We must have been out there for half an hour. I told Mary I'd seen Colin screwing this other girl. I didn't know, yet, who it was. I hated that word, screwing. I said, 'Screw, screw, screw the lot of you,' and the anger and tears and hurt were all jumbled up again.

She said, 'If I were you, I wouldn't walk away, run away from it. I'd go back to the party, go into the room and say, 'What the hell do you think you're doing?' I laughed at that, a cracked laugh with tears floating all around it, but the thought of walking into the midst of their passion was too much. I said, 'You must be crazy.'

We were standing in the roadway having this weird conversation. Mary was saying, 'Are you scared? Are you scared what might happen if you went back?'

'I'm not scared at all,' I said. I was thinking then, 'Why doesn't she leave me alone?' I said, 'The point is that we believe in free love; if Colin wants to go and sleep with another woman, then he can. I've no right to stop him. I don't own him after all, I mean we're both free people.'

'Then why are you crying?' Mary said. 'If you have it all so well worked out, why cry?'

'I'm crying because I'm tired. I've had ... I don't know. I'm just so nervy all the time...' Stop, I thought. Stop telling this woman. She'll only laugh at you later. They were all the same. They'd listen to you and say *There, there*, and then off to bed with your man if they got half a chance. They really liked it if they thought they'd comforted you beforehand. Made it spicier.

Mary was saying, 'Oh poor, bloody women. Always eating their hearts out trying to be cooler and more sophisticated than the doll next door and cracking up in the process.'

I said, 'I'm not cracking up,' and my voice sounded exactly as if I was.

Mary took my arm and said, 'Come back in and have a drink. Maybe if you say Boo! to the monster he'll turn out to have feet of clay.'

I was just going to say, very snotty, 'Look I don't need your advice thank you,' or something like that, and then I thought, 'Well why not? It's better than going home to that flat and waiting for Colin to come in. Why not indeed?' So the two of us started walking back to the nightmare party.

By the time we'd returned, the party faces had slipped a bit. The girls were getting tipsy. Girls always seem to get tipsy quicker than men, but then they don't get that evil, black drunk men get sometimes.

Girls just open their faces; their faces grow greasy and their pores open up and their eyes go smaller, swimmier, and their mouths bigger and they look up at men and you'd think some of them were just asking to be smashed.

Mary went off to get some drinks and I thought, Please let her stay with me and not go off with some guy. Please.

Angus came over. 'Having little girly chats in the loo then?' he said, a stupid, drunken smile on his face.

'Oh Angus, piss off,' I said. 'Why don't you just leave me alone.' Angus looked. His eyes went black, like pinheads in his big white face. Then he smiled, 'Oh dear, cranky tonight, are we darling?' I said, 'Fuck you Angus.' I said it quietly first, just mouthing the words, tasting them. Then I said it louder. I said it and saw the party faces turning, turning—Who *is* this? I said, 'Fuck you Angus.' Angus turned on his heel and walked away. I could hear my voice; it went up to the ceiling like a hard blot and then came down again; it went round and round the room, laughing.

That was the first time I ever said, 'Fuck you' to anybody. In public. I was standing on my own, watching the faces and bodies, and it was like looking through the end of a telescope—they'd all gone distorted and tiny.

Mary said, 'Have a drink.'

We sat down on a sofa. Luckily I had one of those faces that didn't show up all blotchy and red after tears; it just went sort of whiter and thinner. I was shaking again. Mary said 'What happened?' I told her I'd shouted at Angus. She just said, 'About time too.' Some of the people looked at us sitting there but by that stage I didn't care.

Mary started talking about what she did in the telly. Something about Light Entertainment shows, she kept saying 'LE'— that was what they called Light Entertainment. I wasn't listening very much. I was drinking and wondering what I was going to do when Colin came out. I thought, I'll go in like Mary says. I'll just walk in and say, 'May I inquire what you two animals are up to?' I thought, That will sound laughable. Colin will just laugh. They'll both laugh. They'll be clutching each other, clutching breasts and penises and hair and saying, 'Ha, ha, do go away little girl, nobody really wants you here, just go back to the nursery and play with your toys—there's a good girl.'

I was beginning to get drunk. Systematically. I was thinking of forests inside my head. Dark forests where the trees met overhead and you ran and ran and never got out. I was thinking of a clown at a circus once, when I was a kid. His face all white with big red tears painted down his cheek. He used to ask us to come and sit on his knee and he'd tickle the girls, and his hands were like iron, tickling. After the show once he put his hand up my knickers behind a caravan and I went white inside and ran and never told anyone. I was thinking of rivers. I was thinking of a lake in Glendalough that had a hard, flat, grey face. It was held up on a rack between three mountains. It never moved. Just this flat, grey, face looking up at the sky. I was thinking of Father and Mary sitting in that house with the stiff-legged, unblinking dolls waiting and watching upstairs. I was thinking of Colin and why did I stay with him, why? And thinking it was because of definition, something to do with being told to do this and do that, a reassurance.

Ruth and a man joined us. He was an artist. He had a very long face. Long like a horse's, and his lips were rubbery, they moved separately, up and down. He was saying, 'I'd like to paint you some day, you've a beautiful face, a beautiful Irish face with all that black hair and those green-brown eyes and that marvellous white skin … mmm.' I thought, any minute now he's going to lick me, like an ice cream.

We were sitting on the floor. He passed round a joint. Ruth was very drunk; she was saying, 'Marshall McLuhan will replace Jesus in the spiritual consciousness of Western civilization.' She was looking at the artist as she was saying it. He would just say, 'Yeah, sure Ruthy.' He wasn't interested in her, much. He was getting into himself on the pot. Going very quiet, still.

Mary didn't smoke. She said, 'I'm part of the Booze Culture,' and Ruth and this artist (I can't remember his name) just looked at her with their eyes glassy, and you could see they were thinking, Who is this creep refusing to play the game? I was thinking, God how is it that human beings can sometimes be so awful to each other? Colin would say, That is the morbidity induced by too much gin.

I was looking around the room at all the girls and thinking of this story I was told once about a French king who dressed up all these dolls in the latest French fashions, high couture, and sent them round the world at vast expense to show what the latest Parisian designs were. I thought, That's what we women are like. I told Ruth and Mary and the artist about the French king. I said, 'Don't you think that's what we're like—fashion dolls?' The artist said, 'Weird, absolutely far round.'

Somebody put on some music. There were only about twenty people left. No Colin. I thought, They're asleep in there by now, must be. Couldn't still be going. Asleep in each other's arms. Sweaty and warm. Her damn eyes. Did she keep her eyes open during it?

Angus came over and asked Mary to dance. She went off and I nearly panicked. I wanted to scream out. I thought, Keep dancing, that's the main thing.

Somebody put on 'Zorba the Greek'. The sounds were long, like hunting horns over fields and fields of land—long, streaming sounds.

I could feel the music as if it were being played through me. The artist got up and started to dance; he was saying, 'Dance, lovely lady, dance.' His voice was like a snake's: *Dance, dance.* We started dancing to each other, our bodies touching and moving and whirling in great curves of light and sound to the music, and he was lifting me up on a table, a low round table, and dancing round the table, the music was going faster then, the drums were in my head, and I was the music …

I was wearing this silk shirt and silk trousers, and I was lifting the shirt and feeling the air on my belly, and the shifting of my skin and I felt I was part of the centre of the earth, I was life, and I was pulling the shirt further and then unbuttoning it and the artist was dancing, his head rolling on his shoulders; he was saying, 'Yeah, yeah,' and I could see more people watching, and they were all dancing round the table, sighing and moving, and the music was slowing again and I was undoing the zip on my trousers and letting them fall, fall …

… and my hands went up to my breasts and I was dancing just in my pants and the music was going faster, faster, and the people were going, *Ahh, ahh,* and I was swirling now, drunk; my body was gold, it was water, it was the moon melting under the sun, and dancing and dancing, and the artist was touching and hands were stretching out and touching, and touching, and I thought, I'll dance for you all, I'll dance for the pain and the sorrow and …

Colin's face at the kitchen door. Colin's white face. Colin running. Colin shouting. Hitting the artist in his beard and a little mess of teeth and blood. Colin purple in the face. Colin shouting, 'Get down Elizabeth, get down.' Colin ripping his jacket off wrapping it round me, wrapping and rough, like I was never going to be opened again. Mary's face. Smiling. Mary saying, 'See you round kiddo,' or something like that.

ىچ ىچ

PART THREE

We were sitting in a pub. It was about eight o'clock. A July evening. Colin and I had driven in from the park where he had been doing some film location work. The evening sun had made the tops of the grass look like gleaming fish. Shoals of gleaming fish.

Colin was edgy. Starting to get drunk. Pints of Guinness and doubles of whiskey. Pints and chasers.

Mary and Ruth came in with a group of ballad singers with whom they had just done a recording session for one of Mary's Light Entertainment shows. The ballad singers wore pointy black shoes and tight trousers and their legs were white and hairy between their trouser bottoms and short socks. They kept elbowing each other and giving shouts of laughter and saying, 'Jaysus lads, d'ya remember that one?' One of them said to Ruth, 'Are ya not going to introduce us to Miss Gorgeous here?' Ruth laughed and said, 'This is Elizabeth, Colin Dempsey's girlfriend.' We all shook hands then, and the one who had asked gave an extra-long shake.

Colin said, 'And what are we all having?' and ordered up pints and chasers for everyone. Ruth said, 'Colin *really*.' She knew the mood as well.

Colin and Ruth were sitting beside one another. They were talking about something in the station; Ruth was going, *Nnh, nnh,* and nodding her head. Looking at Colin very earnestly, very attentive. Bitch, I thought, interested in each other's minds indeed.

I knew the mood well. It would be more drink and then dinner in some restaurant and hopefully a party afterwards. If not it would be a discotheque. Home at five, exhausted, drunk through almost to soberness, poised like a knife, waiting for a fight, pushing for one.

We fought so much now. Not like the fights when we first started living together. Shouting and banging things and then jumping into bed and tears and sex for hours. Now we fought dry, hard fights. Ever since the party, things had been cracking up.

I hadn't spoken to Colin for three days after it. I went and stayed with Mary. I'd no plans or anything, I just thought, I'll get out for a bit. Mary was working very hard so I didn't see very much of her. Then late one night Colin came round. He was terribly drunk, banging on the door and shouting. He came into my room and shut the door and put a chair under the handle and forced me down on the bed and lay on top of me and cried, and said I was never to leave him, and to love him, and then I started crying too, and we lay like children in the bed, holding on to each other and crying. The next day I went back to his flat.

Then there was this business about the psychiatrist. Colin arranged for me to go and see one. He said, 'Anyone who makes an exhibition of themselves like you did at that party needs to see a bloody headman.' Well I wasn't sure about this psychiatrist; I didn't think the stripping thing was so awful. You get high and you get sad and you do funny things. Not madness. But whenever I started arguing with Colin he'd always win and I'd end up crying and not knowing what I'd meant to say.

The psychiatrist was about thirty-five with this sallow, wet-looking face and long fiddly fingers. His office, or consulting room, or whatever you call it, was completely bare, not a picture, nothing. Just a desk where he sat and a wooden chair for the patient.

He said, 'Well now, what seems to be the trouble?'

I was very taken aback. I thought they were supposed to tell you what the trouble was.

I thought, I'm in here in the nut house because I'm a flasher. I started giggling. I couldn't stop. This psychiatrist's face went all stiff, like sour cream. I thought, If they want me to act mad then mad I will be.

I said, 'Every time I go into a room where there are a lot of men I get this desire to strip. I want to let them see how beautiful my body is, even if they can't touch it.' I said, 'Nobody touched me much when I was a child,' and then this wave of self-pity came and I burst into tears and left his office.

I told Colin I wasn't going back. It was the first time I think that I completely refused to do something he wanted. I just said,

'No. I'm not going back.' I went out of the flat and walked down to the sea and was shaking.

Colin was angry for days afterwards. It wasn't the damn psychiatrist; it was just me saying no. Even still I could win sexually. He'd sit up late pretending to read and refusing to answer anything I said. I'd go and sit at his knee and start stroking him and feeling him coming up and sometimes we'd make love right on the floor.

I kept thinking, It will get better, it will, it will. And still I felt there was absolutely nothing I could do to make it better. I got really fanatical about my body, bathing it, creaming it. Colin would watch sometimes when I was in the bathroom. I was standing in front of this long mirror one day and he was sitting behind me. He got up and came over and our glass eyes met in the mirror. He said, 'All women love themselves, especially beautiful ones.' He started stroking me, stroking my breasts and belly and then down, and he made me come, standing there, the two of us looking in the mirror and my legs were trembling. Afterwards he laughed; he said, 'There, I told you, you're more excited by your own bodies than by men's.'

Mary said, 'That's true.' She said, 'We're all so bombarded with sexy images of the female body, on every hoarding, in every magazine, that it's surprising men aren't leaping on women in the street and raping them. The poor buggers must go round with erections most of the time.'

'If you say, "Mary said" once again,' Colin shouted when I told him that, 'I'll hit you over the bloody head. I'm sick of hearing Mary said this, and Mary said that. Fuck Mary.'

I said, 'Maybe she wouldn't like that.' He threw a book at me.

I liked Mary. I think she was the first woman I really liked. She was so calm. She wasn't like most women who narrow their eyes and go hate, hate, as soon as a new woman comes along. She'd say Hello, and ask them what they were doing, or whatever. You felt she was interested. Also she didn't change when men were around; not like those women who talk to you about this and that and then a man turns up and you'd think they were a different person. Oh I'd done it myself. I knew the tricks. Mary was never like that.

I used to go and see her at the television station whenever I went to collect Colin.

I used to talk to her a lot about Colin. Those three days I spent at her flat I was trying to tell her why seeing Colin in bed with that girl had been so awful. It was something you could think about in your mind and say, 'Well of course we're liberated, and don't mind little things like that,' and so on. You could accept it in your head. But finding him there with her, seeing him do the same things as he did with you, going over and over it in your head …

Colin didn't like Mary. He couldn't understand a very attractive woman who didn't respond to him sexually. I think that was it. Colin was the Wham, Bam, Thank you Ma'am type. He said he was sexually liberated, free. He said if he fancied a girl, he'd give her the eye, she'd concede, or not, and they'd go to bed and have sex. That was the end of that. Unless she was really good in bed in which case it might last a bit longer. But no strings attached, he'd say. I'd seen one or two girls falling for him. Heard the chat. 'Do you believe in free love? Come on then, darling, don't be such a square, whip off your panties and bow down to the great age of permissiveness.' Some girls! You'd think they wanted to be trampled on, *oh yes, yes*, and off to the slaughter house—and the next day feeling all crumpled inside. Feeling like tarts and never being able to understand why.

We were talking about this in the pub. Free love and all that. Mary said, 'Free love, my arse. It's a bloody myth, man-made of course, to keep the sex thing going their way. All the little dollies desperate to show they're hip and modern and dropping their drawers for any hick passing by. Free indeed.'

Colin said in this very snotty voice, 'So what, my dear Mary, is free love?' His face was blotchy, belligerent.

Mary said, '"Free" means, I think, being independent. If both the man and the woman were independent, if one didn't crave security through establishing the omnipotence of his penis and the other didn't crave security by giving up everything and attaching her lifeline to that penis, then you might get your free love.'

The ballad singers had gone very quiet at this stage. Colin was laughing and going, Ha, ha, but you could see he was searching around for something cutting, a little bonk on the head for the brave Mary.

'I'm not saying'—Mary paused and looked into her glass, and then looked up at Colin—'I'm not saying that it's only women who suffer from our fucked-up sex lives, but women suffer more.'

'Would you say a twenty-five-year-old man could have free love with a seven-year-old girl? Well most women's emotional and intellectual development stops when they're seven. That's when they reach the Age of Reason. That's when they give up the unequal struggle, accept that coquetry, nattering, cock-sucking and cock-teasing are the tools of their trade, their weapons for survival. If that's your famous free love—you can stuff it.'

Mary got up and said she was going to the Ladies'. Her back was stiff. It was like a cat's back when it's angry. Arched.

One of the ballad singers said, 'Well I dunno I'm sure, women is gettin' terrible peculiar these days.'

'Bloody lesbian,' Colin said. He was trying to pretend it was nothing. His hand shook as he reached for a cigarette. I was just sitting and watching and listening. Very quiet. Frightened.

When Mary came back she was quite calm again. She said, 'I've got a terrible habit of making speeches.' She bought everyone a drink. She said, 'If I sing will you join in?' The ballad singers were delighted with relief. They had all been sitting stiff. Their buttocks shifting on the leatherette seats, squeaking; looking up at the ceiling, laughing, and then silence and then shifting and squeezing their buttocks again on the seats.

Mary sang a long lonely ballad about this girl who loves a butcher boy and is going to have a baby and hangs herself in a bedroom because it's all hopeless. She half closed her eyes and was feeling the words as they came out: a strong, smooth, oaken sound.

The ballad singers were saying, 'Good on you girl' and 'Arraigh leat.' I thought, If I start to cry now I'll never stop. I wanted to hold Colin's hand and tell him I loved him, and that we would be okay, and that everything would be all right between us for ever and ever.

'*You stoooopid bitch!*'

Colin's face was twisted. I jumped up. I had been crossing my legs and hit the table, knocking over a pint. There was Guinness everywhere. All down Ruth's dress. The table awash. The ashtray with butts and ash floating. Colin's eyes had gone tiny; he looked like a snake, his mouth poisonous, those tiny black eyes.

I said, 'For God's sake Colin, it was a mistake, I didn't mean to spill the bloody drink.' I was standing up and Guinness was dripping down like black blood. I was shaking all over.

He said, 'Don't shout and don't use that language.' 'Bugger off,' I said. 'Just leave me alone.' Colin was half standing too, ready to hit. I thought, If he hits me now I'll hit him back, as hard as I can, I'll hit him with all that I am.

We were both standing there; it must have been just for a minute but it was a minute that ballooned out into hugeness.

Colin said, 'Oh piss off.' He picked up his drink. I suddenly felt very cold. I thought, Hate will be my strength; it will carry me through.

I said, 'I'm going now.' I could hear my voice coming from a long way off. A mountaintop voice. I said, 'I'm going back to the flat to collect my things. I never want to see you again.'

I picked up my bag. The car keys, cigarettes. The ballad singers were all looking at the floor, their shoes, the ground, anywhere. Only Mary watched. She didn't say anything. Ruth was holding Colin's arm. He was screaming. I didn't hear. The words were coming at me and I thought: They'll hurt later, it will all hurt later, like after an accident they say you're numb at first and then the pain starts deep in the wounds and gradually possesses you, nerve cell by nerve cell. Later, I thought, later, and the words just kept coming.

∽ **2** ∽

Mary said, 'Okay. You can stay the night, but tomorrow you'll have to start looking for a flat of your own.'

Tomorrow. I'll do everything tomorrow. Just let me sleep now. Let me rest. I was sitting on her sofa between piles of newspapers, books, files. An advertisement in this magazine said, 'We want to make you useful … even interesting.' The phrase kept clanging round in my head.

I was still folding my case. I couldn't remember what I'd put into it. I remember standing at the cupboard in the flat thinking I could stand there forever. Then the phone rang. I didn't answer it. But suddenly I began to move, to stuff things into the case. I kept running backwards and forwards taking things, then dropping them. What would I take? What would I need?

It was an odd assortment. Two evening dresses (in case somebody asks you out); a shirt of Colin's (a memento), a picture (he might sell everything when you've gone), a doll (comfort for the long nights), two books: *How to Keep the Body Beautiful* and *The Faber Book of Modern Verse* (for the long, long days).

Mary made a cup of tea. She didn't say anything. I thought, For God's sake I wish she'd say something—anything. Even, 'Why don't you go back to him?' I would have gone.

It was midnight. I must have spent a long time looking in that damn cupboard. How pain changes time. An hour becomes a yawning chasm, a night a full stop between what was and what is going to be. A gap between your action and its consequences.

I'd sat in the car outside the flat with the suitcase in the back wondering where to go. I hadn't wanted to go to a hotel. I couldn't go home. I thought of David and then thought, 'You can't use people that much; they'll turn on you.' I thought of Valerie, but I didn't want to be told about different men for different moods. I thought then of Mary. I thought, Mary will know what to do.

'So what do you do now?' Mary said. She was sitting on the floor, cross-legged.

I thought, I shouldn't have come here. David would have hugged me; he would have said, 'It's all right old girl.' Something. Why was she so cold?

Mary said, slowly, not to me, sort of to the room: 'If you can't get along with your lover you can always get out of his bed, but what do you do when your country is fucking you over?' She laughed. 'Who said that?' I didn't know. Didn't care.

I started to cry. I thought, I'm alone now, completely alone. At least Colin was there. At least he was mine, part of me. We were

Colin and Liz, a unit. A something. I felt, Now I'm a nothing. I'm just a piece of pain.

'Don't cry,' Mary said. 'There's no point in crying. Women are always bloody crying. It means you don't have to think. You fuddle up your brain with tears and pain and go, *Oh, oh,* and wait for a man to come along and pick up the pieces.'

She was walking up and down the room now. I wanted her to stop. Be quiet. Let me have the pain, let me alone.

She went on: 'If you want to go back to Colin, then go. You know now what it means, living with him. You don't have to pretend any more. It can be good and bad. It's not a dream, not a romance of Coca Cola and ever-so-fresh and non-stop kissing and hugging and fresh coffee and rolls in the morning. You know him. Go back to him if you realize that. If you don't then you'll have to start building your own life.'

She was standing in front of me. The words were spinning in my head, spinning and then dropping into this enormous void. Building your own life ... decide ... pretend ...

She said, 'One thing is sure. You're not going to stay here and weep on me and then go running back to Colin the first time he asks you.'

I stood up. I said, 'I'll go now. I just thought you could help me, that's all—I just thought I could stay here for a few days.' I had this weird sensation of sorrow at the sound of my own voice, such a sad, cracked voice.

Mary put her hand out; she said, 'Look I'm sorry Liz, I'm sorry, you must be exhausted.'

❦ 3 ❦

I was turning over, the warmth of the blankets around me, the womb warmth of sleep ... stretching ... then looking up and seeing the light bulb hanging over my head ... and then ...

Where am I?

...and then the hurt creeping in, seeping in like in a wound. I was alone. I'd left Colin. The bed was so narrow. So single. I turned over on my stomach, that way it ached less, the lack of another body, the gap around my body, its nakedness to the whole world's laughing and pinching and horrors.

Such an emptiness … but the pain begins to fill that until you think you'll scream, till you think you'll destroy yourself with your pain; that your being and its being cannot go on together. One or the other must die or win. Your eyes are dry then; you can't imagine ever crying—crying seems warm, crying seems like a river, not this—with this you could never cry; this is a bleaching and stretching and yawning until you exist only in the perimeters of your body, on the very surface of your skin, until you are made of glass and the top of your head has been sliced off like a boiled egg's and air and wind are rushing in. Painfully.

∞ 4 ∞

Discreet, gay, professional gentleman seeks civilized companion (m. or f.) to share 3 room k&b flat, Rathgar area.

I toyed with the idea. Could I match his discreet gayness with my well-bred civilizedness?

But no. It was serious. Everything was serious. I had to have a job and a place to live. Both. Mary and I went through all the papers together.

Bedsit, eve. meal incl. £3 pw. Sandymount. I thought of the evening meal sitting hugely in the centre of a brown linoleum room—like a Magritte painting. I crossed that one off the list.

I answered one ad asking for *4th girl to share spacious flat (own rm.) Donnybrook area* (the posh ads always said 'area').

The three girls, looking for a fourth, said they'd be delighted to show me their flat that evening. I took the bus over. Odd humiliating things like that nearly kill you; you get used to a car and to money, and each time you go out you're reminded you're without them and you hate buses like hell. The car belonged to Colin and I'd left it outside the television station with a note and the keys. Mary said I should have kept it until I found a flat and things but that was worse.

The three girls sat on a divan bed in the living room. They said they were Amanda, Jo (for Josephine), and Anne. They giggled. The living room was used by one of the girls as her bed-room when everyone else had gone to bed. They took turns in the living room, they said. They giggled again. They interrupted each other.

They said, 'Somebody does the launderette once a week (we all wash our own undies), and somebody does the cooking, and somebody does the washing up, and we have a list, here, see, so nobody has to do all the work, it's all planned …'

They showed me my separate bedroom. It had a single bed and a wardrobe that went from the floor almost to the ceiling. The linoleum was vomit pattern. The bathroom had three rows of tights and pants and yellowing bras hanging on sodden string lines over the bath. There was a shelf with half-finished bottles of cream on it and scattered powder and a broken lipstick case and a sanitary towel and two boxes of Tampax. (Colin once saw an ad in an American paper that said, 'Tampax! Almost as good as the Real Thing'.)

The three girls said, 'Stay for supper.' That was to suss me out. A boyfriend came. He sat in a chair and the girls all giggled at him and the one who was his girlfriend wouldn't speak to him but sulked in a chair. Then she went out and had a confab with one of the other girls in the passageway. She came back in and said, 'Come on' and she and her spotty boyfriend went into one of the bedrooms. We could hear the bed creaking through the partition walls.

I said I wanted to go to the bathroom. I locked the door and climbed out of the window and ripped my bloody tights. I thanked God it was a ground floor flat and ran down the street, hating those girls and pitying them and thinking of the rooms ro-tating and launderettes rotating in weekly cycles. Mary thought it was a scream.

Landladies look at you. They say, 'On your own dear?' They try to make out if you're pregnant or if you're on the run from someone or something or if you're a prostitute. Landladies hate girls.

Landladies like the boys and the men with their dirty socks and late drunken nights and meals of beans eaten from the tins.

They can scold and patronize and go Tsch, tsch, such poor neglected boys. Girls are sneaky; they say that girls put san towels and hair down the lavs and block them, and then the landladies' husbands have to come and clear them. Girls spill nail varnish on the Good Carpet.

You go through the papers first thing in the morning. You make phone calls. You say, 'When could I come and see it?' You ask the rent.

They let you in the door; they show you the room. It's always worse than you imagined; it's always mean and yellowed and rubbed against by so many bodies; the curtains are heavy with the sighs and tiny despairs of the bedsitter population that's lived there. It smells of onions and cabbage and unwashed bodies.

The landladies look at you. They don't mind if you don't like the room. They look at you. You say, 'Umm, does this window open by any chance?' You make your voice gentle, polite. You try not to grunt as you push at the only window in the kitchenette. The window doesn't open. None of them ever open.

I thought, Why did I leave Colin? Why did I leave that beautiful flat by the sea? I thought of walking out of that pub and my strength then. I thought, Hate will be my strength—it carried me through packing and going, but then I got tired. The papers made me tired. The landladies with their damned eyes made me tired. I thought I'd scream if another one asked me what sort of job I had, what my father did; probe, probe, probe till I wanted to say, 'I am a whore to end all whores. My father is a gigolo. Nightly he will bring at least a score of men to my room where they will take their pleasure of my body. We will writhe and scream and spit in the face of God … now, can I see the flat *please*?'

At first I thought of all the good things with Colin—times when we'd laughed and put on diamond faces for each other and danced for each other. I thought of him saying, 'Yeah, that looks good on you. Christ you really do look something tonight,' and feeling his eyes, his pleased eyes, looking at me. That made me beautiful.

I thought of him talking to his friends. His hands patting the words down, excited words. I thought of him working, leaping down from the gantry to the studio floor: 'No this way'—his looking through the camera lens, a stopwatch swinging from his neck.

I thought of him in bed. His sureness. His hands like china, hands so smooth and sure. His body like wire. His concentration on me. The way he'd say, 'We'll make you oblivious,' and go round and round me till I was all sensation, all feeling, a total nerve ending, and then he'd come into me.

But then there were the bad things I remembered. Watching him flirting with girls. That feeling of his power over me. How he could make me oblivious and how awful it was to see him preparing other people for that. At the time it had been me and him; it was personal between us and I felt annihilated at the thought of him doing it with somebody else.

The days in the flat: waiting my life away from the time when he left till the time he came back. Listening to records. Making clothes, doing something to my body. Making something to eat. The days stretched and contracted around him; long days if he worked, short if he stayed at home.

The ache to be approved of. Anything, I'll do anything, if only you'll tell me I'm okay. The wondering: Does he love me? Will he leave me? Aren't there lots of other girls with sexier bottoms, and bigger bosoms? Even the ugly ones, aren't they potentially dangerous as well? He might fall for a really ugly one.

Feeling scared. Not something I could even think about very much. I kept it in a box. Locked. But wondering sometimes, What am I doing? I'm doing nothing. I can't do nothing, I can't. Somebody is going to come and ask me one day, 'Why are you doing nothing?'

Colin said, 'That's your bloody Catholic conscience again.' It didn't stop the scared feeling. What if he leaves? What if I get fat, or spotty, or old? But that's not the important thing. Who am I without him now? I danced for him till my legs ached; if he goes whom will I dance for? People will laugh at me dancing down the streets like a madwoman, all on my own.

Mary said that being on my own would be the worst thing in the beginning. But it would improve. Would it? The world suddenly seemed such a hollow vault. My footsteps echoing round and round echo in my mind, soft grey marks astronauts might leave on the moon. Everything seemed grey. The colours had been sucked back into somebody's head.

Why? Why leave?

It was that shout in the pub: 'You stupid bitch.' I felt a curtain come down inside my head. I thought, Right, that's it. You'll never shout at me like that again. I didn't think, I'm very clever and therefore you shouldn't shout, or, I'm very beautiful and you shouldn't shout. I just thought, I'm a person; you mustn't ever shout at me like that again. I thought, I'm something. I must find out what. I must go back and then go forward. Reopen some doors.

The doors were stiff. Doors to the past and doors to the future. Thinking about it. Planning it. Wondering, What next? Where do I go from here? Looking for a flat in the summer days.

The flat was finally a room. The room was an attic. The attic was in the roof of a pub looking over the River Liffey.

The man said, 'Fifty bob a week, shared bathroom and kitchen with meself and the missus, and a drink on the house at Christmas.' The man was called Mr Maloney. At first he was very reserved. Mary said, 'It's your accent.' He'd stand behind the bar in a filthy apron, his flecked nose matching the marble-top counter. Gradually, though, he became more friendly. Offered me a nightcap, or an evening shot. 'Oiling the works for the night's endeavours,' he'd say. He'd say, 'A terrible dirty life, surely.' He said it as if he didn't mean it; a sort of refrain. His wife was an invalid. She stayed upstairs in a dark bedroom with the curtains closed.

Mary helped me move in. We painted the room white and I polished up a big old brass bed and she gave me a huge rug to put over it.

My first night in Maloney's I went down to use the loo. It was about ten o'clock. We'd been painting all day and I was exhausted. I could hear the voices downstairs in the bar, like an orchestra tuning up, loud voices and soft voices and a purple sort of rumbling.

The loo was at the end of this long corridor. It had once been a bathroom but Mr Maloney had sold the bath so there was just this very old loo on a sort of dais at the end of a narrow, long room. There was no lock on the door. You couldn't sit on the lav and keep your foot against the door at the same time; it was too far away. I thought, What the hell, nobody is going to come up here at this hour.

I sat down and was in full flight when the door started opening.

A red blotchy man's face wobbling on top of a dark suit peered in. The door opened a bit further. The man's face opened into a wide smile. More faces appeared. More smiles. I just sat on peeing. There was nothing else I could do. I smiled back. The faces gave forth a little grinning cheer. I stood up and they all discreetly left. It was the first time I'd really laughed in weeks. Maloney had forgotten to tell me that sometimes he let one of the rooms upstairs for conferences, meetings.

∽ 5 ∽

The first four days I didn't leave my room in the pub. I just went out to get milk, bread and cigarettes. I ate the bread dry and drank cup after cup of coffee. I slept and then woke and had coffee and then slept again. I went out with a long coat on over my nightdress to get the milk and the bread. I thought, Ah, if only the girls could see me now. If only Colin could see me now. I imagined being found dead on my polished brass bed. 'Ex-model found dead on brass bed—ex-boyfriend heartbroken.'

Then a Sunday had come. The bell of the church just down the road was cracked. It made an odd cracking echo, calling the people to Mass. I sat at my attic window and looked down at the women in their nylon scarves and shapeless coats and flat shoes pushing against the wind to get to the church. I saw a drunk from the night before (from forever?) bang-clattering along the pavement. Two seagulls painted white curves of light over the sluggish river.

I thought, One more day in this room and I'll go daft in the head.

I came to Mary's. I was rummaging through my bag looking for money and suddenly remembered David's cheque. It was still there. I'd told Mary about it, about the afternoon in the hotel. She was laughing till tears came down her face. She said, 'Why don't you go and cash it?' We'd had this argument about the cheque. I said I didn't think it was right to do it, oh, because David was pitiful or something. She was saying, 'Well if he's rich why be so worried about it?'

I put the cheque back in the zipper pocket and thought, Well I'll keep it as insurance; if things get really bad I can cash it.

I realize now why I'd come to Mary—for help. Somebody to say, 'Look, why don't you try this, or this, or that?'

We talked for hours—well it was mostly Mary talking. She talked about women, how she really feels for women, how banjaxed they are. She told me about this woman friend of hers who put her head in the gas oven because her husband ran off with a seventeen-year-old girl. The husband came back and found her and dragged her out screaming to the hospital. He used to come and visit her and she'd know this lovely girl would be tapping impatiently outside the door. When she came out of the hospital she packed her things and went to a cottage in the country and didn't see anyone for six months. She began painting. She painted herself back to sanity.

She talked about me. What would I do? What? I could go back to modelling. She said she thought that would be ridiculous. She said, 'It's time you stopped being a bloody clothes-horse; it's time you stopped worrying what other people think of you and start thinking what you want to be yourself.'

She said the only way to go forward is to go back. She said you must go back to the dead, still centre of yourself, just being calm, if you can, and thinking, and slowly building up on what you have, not what other people give you, or refuse you.

I wanted her to be my friend. I wanted to stay with her, to have her look after me. I wanted her to go on talking to me about women and their problems, and the way she saw things, like jealousy and bitchiness between women; the way she explained them. The way she said, 'Look, emotions aren't the only thing.

There's the whole world in a state of chaos. There's work to be done.'

What would I work at? What would I do? She said a typing course was the first thing. Being a secretary wasn't much but at least it was a start. She said that it would bring in the bread and butter and then I could start looking around. We were sitting in the flat smoking and I was thinking of looking, looking around the world I suppose for the first time and thinking, What could I do? And that being quite a good, strong feeling.

Mary knew of this typing school; a friend of hers ran it. They did a crash touch-typing course. You wouldn't need shorthand. Everyone had Dictaphones now. We rang up the friend and I was to start the next day.

Then there was money. I had thirty pounds when I left Colin. Mary had lent me some more. She rang another friend, a girl who worked in a restaurant. The girl said she'd ask the boss the following night if he'd take on somebody else. She said, 'I'm sure he will, a girl left only two weeks ago to have a baby and we haven't replaced her.'

We made lunch: bacon and beans and bread and a bottle of red wine. I was starving; it was the first time in years I'd eaten without thinking, Oh Jesus is this going to make me fat?

You think of the whole world working. Most people working at jobs they despise. Getting up at 7.30; scraping yesterday's food and cigarette tar off their teeth, last night's sleep off their faces, depositing yesterday's waste matter down the toilet, filling their stomach with more; clothing their bodies; catching their train, or their bus, or bicycle, or driving their car; spending the best part of their waking lives, their years, behind a desk, beside a conveyor belt, underneath a machine. It was frightening.

We were sitting at the table in the kitchen with the wine and warmth and food keeping the world out.

'You won't be rescued,' Mary said. She said it in a kind, slow voice. I felt panic rising: stop, stop telling me horrible things—tomorrow, I'll think about it tomorrow.

She said, 'Before it was easy for you. Colin did everything. He earned money for both of you, he thought for both of you, he made decisions for both of you—you've told me he even bought your clothes.'

I said, 'No. He helped me choose them.' 'Did you ever go on wearing something he didn't like?' I said, 'Yes, of course.' But I hadn't. Of course. I didn't feel the tears coming; I was just suddenly aware of them pouring down my face. They were tears for me, for Colin, for Mary, for the woman who'd put her head in the gas oven, for the women who didn't but would have liked to. I supposed mostly they were for me—the jobs, the bedsitters, the life, the flat, flat life stretching ahead of me—nobody going to rescue me ... nobody. Mary said, 'Talk about it, talk it out of your system,' and we started again.

6

'Like to come for a drink, darling, when you're finished?' The man patted my behind, pat, pat, like you would a sleek pony's. 'I don't drink actually,' I said, emphasizing the *actually* in my frosty waitress voice, hard and thin. You learn the voice quick. It's the only way to protect yourself and them. Sometimes, though, you feel like dumping a plate of wild duck a l'orange over their damn fat heads.

At least I got the job. Mary's friend had rung her the next day and told me to come in for an interview. She said, Tell her to put on something sexy; Peter is really a dirty old man, and he likes his girls to look whorey.'

The other girls told me how to survive from the first night I arrived. They said, 'Be firm, never be snotty, otherwise you won't get a tip, or they might complain to old head-the-ball (Peter, the owner). Just say, "No thanks dear," and carry on clearing the plates. Give them a bit of a wink or something. Lead them on; let them feel they're the sexiest thing since Rock Hudson, and just carry on clearing the plates.'

The restaurant had a rota of eight girls. We worked four a night; the arranging of the schedule was up to us. Peter had a face that perpetually oozed grease. He planned the menus and sometimes did the cooking if it was something experimental. Most of the time he sat around talking to customers who were waiting for a table or watching us. He said, 'I hire my girls for their looks and keep them on for their endurance.'

We started at 5.30 p.m. Cleaned everything, put fresh flowers on the tables, polished the glasses, cracked white linen tablecloths over the round dinner tables. Each evening I came in, the restaurant seemed to smell of disappointment. We would humour it and dress it and chuck it under the chin and open it up for another night's experience, but always it would be sad again the following day.

It was one of these very expensive, exclusive restaurants. We served the best steaks in town. Everyone said that. You'd see the women coming in and eating steaks and then they'd have three veg and wine and coffee and cheese and go home convinced they'd had a slimming dinner. You got to hate people eating. They were so vulnerable-looking. So ugly. The women all looked at the men and the men looked at other women, going platitude, platitude, and the women thinking they were the greatest thing since fried bread.

At first I used to think the girls were awful, the way they'd smile at the customers and then come into the kitchen and say, 'Jesus! What a poxey lookin' divil,' and splutter with laughing and then stiffen their faces up again like dough and go marching back out with the hors d'oeuvres. After a week you were the same yourself. You'd stand weighted on one leg listening respectfully while the man said what he wanted, and what his girlfriend, or wife or mistress wanted, and let him be pompous; then write it all down and not snigger when he pronounced the wine wrong. Off with you to the kitchen to say, 'Janey Mac!'

For my first week there my feet ached the whole time. I'd peel off my tights as soon as I got home and pull the table over to the sink and sit up on it and drop my painful, blue, swollen feet in and run the cold tap over them. I thought, My feet are like Stilton cheese—soft, blue-white, rotting, smelly.

But the money was good. Two pounds a night, straight, and then whatever you made in tips. It worked out at about four pounds a night. We didn't leave the place till one or two in the morning. So okay, the next day you didn't feel like much and you wanted to get to bed early, but you'd got a good meal and a bit of booze if the customers left some over. I thought, It's better than a lot of other jobs a girl without qualifications could get.

I was doing the typing course during the day and then the restaurant at night, three nights a week, or four, if I could get them. So that was usually twelve pounds a week. It was enough. Sometimes I'd see something in a shop and want it, and want it, and think, Oh God if only I could have that—it was like a pain, the wanting, but mostly it wasn't too bad.

I didn't go out very much the evenings I was off. I'd maybe have a drink down in the pub with Mr Maloney and then go up to my room and read, or go and see Mary. I kept thinking about what she said: 'Nobody's going to rescue you,' and it went round and round my head. I'd feel sick.

You want to be loved. That's the main thing. But you never know whether you're getting it or not. Is it enough, too little, too much? You're a kid and you're being smothered one minute and told to run off and play the next. You say, 'It's not very much that I ask, is it? Just a little love.' You hold your pillow and roll over and say *why?* It seems useless then. You think of all the people you know struggling around in the dark, groping —the sleepwalkers. You're all kids at a party playing blind man's buff but you're always the one with the scarf round your face, your hands stretched out in front of you, looking for something to touch, to hold, to recognize.

I recognized Colin immediately when he came into the restaurant: his sloping shoulders, one slightly higher than the other. He pulled out a chair for the girl to sit on. I was just coming out of the kitchen, two steaks, veg and salad balanced for table number ten. I stopped. Colin had his back to me. He hadn't seen me. I felt as if someone had pulled the chain of a huge lavatory in my head—a tremendous gushing and pouring, almost like a haemorrhage.

They were sitting at one of my tables. One of the girls, Susie, bumped into me from behind. 'Get your finger out, then,' she said and shunted me on. I put the food down in front of the two men and a woman at number ten. One of the men was saying something about a drink. Their voices kept missing my ears. I thought,

If I keep on helping this table, I won't have to turn round. I can just stay here till they go away.

'Could I have the wine list *please?*' the man was saying in this edgy voice. It clicked me back into action. Wine list, wine, order, yessir, of course sir, three barrels full sir and I hope it chokes you. Now, menus for table nine.

'Hello, Colin, hello …'

'My God, Liz! I didn't know you were working here.' Colin had both hands on the edge of the table. His eyes looked enormous, like a cat's eyes at night, luminous.

'Yes,' I said, 'they've made an honest woman of me at last.' I laughed a stiff little constipated laugh. I walked back to the kitchen. The chef said, 'Vassa matter?' The chef was German. He said, 'Here, take dis,' and shoved a glass of port into my hand. I drank it down in one go. The chef did a Charles Atlas stance, biceps flexed, diaphragm pulled in, chest pushed out, his white hat cocked crazily on his head, his striped apron stretched across his belly.

I laughed at this mad German chef who was trying to make me happy. He said, 'Ach, ach, that's better.' He waved his wooden spoon in the air; he said, 'Never say dying till you're dead—an English proverb, no?' I went back through to take their orders.

I hadn't seen Colin for five weeks. Having seen him day and night for a year, lived through him, five weeks seemed the rest of my life. There was *with Colin*, and then *without Colin*. That was all. I hadn't got back or forward to anything else, not really, not yet.

My head felt like a fish bowl. I thought, Everyone will see in. They'll see my frantic thoughts swimming around.

The girl was very pretty. She'd taken a lot of trouble to look that way. I should know. She had curly hair that framed her face, a small pert little nose and glass eyes—mean eyes, I thought. As I was coming back I could hear Colin saying 'Oh from the past you know,' and I wanted to crack their two heads together like eggs.

The girl was having a steak. Colin coq au vin. 'Some wine perhaps?' Oh yes, I thought, a little wine to mellow your edges, a little warm red fluid to blur your eyes, to soften your hurt, to ease your fright, a little wine to help you into bed. A little fool.

Colin ordered a bottle of Pommard. Nothing but the best for

the new lady. The specialness of the first few outings. He looked embarrassed. Good, I thought, let him suffer.

Girls are so dispensable to men. One doesn't fit, so you slip her off and slip on another. There are always plenty of girls waiting for some man to come and slip them on. Pretty girls too. The men move in and out of the pretty girls and gradually they get less pretty as they worry about their fading prettiness and their younger, prettier rivals coming up to sneer at them and flash their pretty young breasts at their own men. Then they cling to them, and the men have to slap them off, to free themselves for other girls; the more they slap the more the girls cling.

I spat in his coq au vin in the kitchen. The chef shouted with laughter. I thought he might have been annoyed; it was, after all, his speciality. He made gestures like peeing into the girl's dish. We laughed a conspirators' laugh and out I went with the dinners.

I thought, What would Mary do in this situation? Each time I came to their table, to take their plates, to pour their wine, to bring their coffee, I wondered what Mary would have done. Mary would be strong, I thought, Mary would think, Fuck you, inside her head, and carry on.

I tried to think, Fuck you, but then my insides were runny and I hated that girl. I thought: You left him, now he's got another girl. Simple. What did you expect? That you'd go back to him, that he'd come running and begging, and you'd go back? Yes, in a way, in many ways, that's what you expected.

He did come round to Mary's flat three times since I'd left. He'd been drunk. He'd called her a hitching, bloody, lesbian whore. He said she'd poisoned my mind against him. He said what she needed was a good fuck. He said she was a know-all whore who wanted to have control over me, to use me for her own ends. Mary said, 'Well what do you expect? The poor man is demented with insecurity.'

Oh I'd thought about going back, often enough. Even went down to the television station one day and then ran back at the last minute. If he'd been there I would have gone with him. Even now, if he jumped up and grabbed my hand and said, 'Let's go, let's run away together for ever and ever,' I would have gone. Back to the flat by the sea. Back to long days. Back to beautiful meals in restaurants. Back to parties with pretty girls. Back to bed. Back to bodies. Even back to hurt, yes, even that.

Colin said, 'Are you allowed to sit down and have a glass of something with us?' He smiled up, so confident, so sure. 'Not while on duty, sir,' I said. And thought, I hate him now, I hate him for that 'us'; once it was 'us'—me and him—now it's another 'us'.

He had a brandy and she had Chartreuse. I thought of the first drink I'd ever had with Colin when I'd asked for Benedictine because it was the only posh drink I knew. Time slid back like a climber falling down the wet-black rock side of a mountain.

I ran into the kitchen and into the chef who was sitting with a glass of wine at the big deal cooking table; I felt an iron fist clenching inside my chest, and my head turning solid, and I could hear my voice saying, 'Oh God, God, God,' and sort of squeaking the words out. The chef's eyes looked like raisins in his puffy white chef's face. He sat me down and pulled my head against his apron, which smelt of a million dinners, and wiped my face with it when I'd stopped crying. Susie came in and said, 'What's wrong?' and I asked her if she would do the bill for number nine. She came back with a note from Colin for me. I burnt it without reading it. Watching it curl and shrivel in the gas flame, I thought, That's that. Now I'm really going to start again.

∽ 7 ∽

We all left the restaurant about 2.00 a.m. I was drunk. Not very, but enough to make me think the road was made of velvet and see despair in the chef's eyes when probably he just had indigestion. Susie and he and I had drunk two bottles of wine between us. They walked down to the river with me and we said goodnight and they went on up the road to the taxi stand.

My little room over the pub. I opened the big heavy door that led up lino-covered stairs to the flats.

Mr Maloney was sitting in his kitchen on the first landing. He was talking to someone, a bottle of whiskey between them on the table. He heard me go by. He came out and said, 'Come in and have a wee scoop with us.' I thought of the room, the sheets, white and cold. I went in.

Mr Maloney poured me a thick yellow glass of whiskey. I don't drink whiskey that often. It burned the back of my throat. I imagined a little soft animal at the back of my throat and the whiskey searing it. Mr Maloney said, 'Yer lookin' terrible sad tonight. Drink up now, there's nothing so bad as a drop of the hard stuff won't cure, or at least alleviate.' He said alleviate with about ten vowels.

He said, 'Miss O'Sullivan is renting the top room offa the missus.' Explaining to his friend. 'Very nice too,' said the friend. (The room or me?)

The friend offered me a Woodbine, saying, 'I don't suppose you'd be after smoking one of these little cancer sticks, would you now?' I said I would. 'Thank you, I would.' Mr Maloney lit it up. We all sat there smoking, me with a new cigarette and they with their small butty ones.

There was a small silence. 'Angels passing,' said Mr Maloney. (A nun had told us that at school: you were supposed to hear the sound of angels' wings during those silences.) I felt sorry I'd interrupted their talk. I couldn't drink the whiskey fast though; I sat sipping it, the whiskey burning and the Woodbine scraping the back of my throat, my head feeling thick.

'A rough night all the same, isn't it?' Mr Maloney said.

I looked up, startled. The night had seemed so smooth—was the smoothness deceptive? But he wasn't asking for an answer.

'A terrible thing them students did to that poor Professor from Africa', said his friend, Mr Hickey.

'Terrible surely,' said Mr Maloney. 'It's a wonder they're not all sent home to England or the North of Ireland, or wherever them heathens come from. Pouring paint over visitin' professors indeed.' They stared down at their glasses of whiskey. The evening paper lay on the table. I hadn't had time to read it before going to work. The headline said 'Students pour paint over professor'. It seemed some of the Maoist students at Trinity had poured red paint over a Professor visiting the College. He was from Salisbury University in Rhodesia. The students said, 'We don't want any fascists here.' I suddenly saw my father's face as he walked out behind the Professor. A surprised face. Some of the paint had gone over his suit too. I felt a jolt. It was suddenly as if I'd never known him. I wanted to laugh too. I could see the students were shouting, shouting their arrogance and their fear and their hate—*fascists go home*—and I could see my father's startled face, surprised at it all. Was he frightened? I couldn't say.

'That's my father,' I said to Mr Maloney and pointed to him. He and his friend were strained over looking at the picture. Mr Maloney took out horn-rimmed glasses.

'Oh now a fine lookin' man surely,' he said. 'I'm sorry for his trouble.' I thought, He's wondering why I don't live at home. He must have assumed up to now that my parents were living in the country or something.

'I don't get on with him actually', I said, believing it as I said it. 'He's just a very different sort of person.' Mr Maloney and his friend nodded. Slightly bewildered. They looked at the picture again. I said, 'I must go now. Thank you very much for the drink.' I tipped back the rest of the whiskey. I thought it wasn't going to go down—like the Egg Flips that Mary used to make me take when I had flu. I always thought they'd come popping up again, *yeeups*.

I went upstairs to my attic. The bed was unmade, clothes hanging from the knobs. They say women living on their own are dirtier than men. They lose their civilized veneer, revert faster. I sat down on the bed and pulled off my shoes, tights, took off my coat. Took out a cigarette, lit it. Thought, I've been smoking too much lately. Puffed coming up the stairs. Puffed at twenty! I thought, Who cares?

I started taking the clothes off the bed. Folding things, jumble-folding. I hung up some dresses in the cupboard. I looked at a long dress Colin had bought for me. It was imitation black satin. Halter-necked and scooped very low at the back. 'That's the first time I've seen one woman with two cleavages,' Angus had said when he'd seen me in it. 'One at the back and one at the front.' I put the dress on. My face looked livid in the mirror, the room untidy and dirty behind the tired face atop a black halter-neck dress.

I washed my face, carefully. Then cleansed it, toned it, and carefully put on make-up. Getting and spending, scraping off and putting on. A recurring theme—the vicious circles of our lives …

I looked in the mirror again. Went over to the long one behind the cupboard door. It was flecked around the edges with black spots of age. Colin once told me what it was that makes mirrors go spotty with age but I couldn't remember what it was.

I put my hand under my hair at the back of my neck, scooped it up and stuck a hairpin in. There was a rose somewhere, a rose made from starched linen that I used to wear. I started throwing things out of the cupboard. 'The rose, where's the damned rose?' It was inside an evening bag, a sleeping rose. I put it in my hair. I put on more eye make-up: wide black lines, deep purple shadows, rouge on my cheeks, powder.

I stood back again from the mirror. Turned, walked away looking over my shoulder, walked back again. I did it again, making my walk sexier, pouting my lips, putting my hands on my hips, elbows strained back, bosom stuck out; I could hear Suzanna's voice: 'Walk as if your body is the most desirable, sexy thing on earth, but no damn fool guy is ever going to get near it … provoke.'

I thought of Mary, her saying once, 'It's easier for you good-looking ones to turn on the sex thing with men always, but therefore very hard for you ever to get through to them, to confront them as real people.' Did I do that? Did I now? Hardly now. I didn't see people. I hadn't been out with a man since Colin. I'd had my bottom pinched in the restaurant, and patted. That was all.

How I'd changed. Five weeks. You look back on it and it just takes a second. Living it seems like years. Five weeks, upon five weeks, upon five weeks. That's your life till you die.

Between now and then you've got to scrape off and put on. You've got to fill up and clean out. You've got to talk. You've got to listen. You won't ever love again. Love? 'What's love,' you say, 'Love is a myth.' It's like religion. It's a bad joke.

Colin said, 'I love you,' he went *Mmm,* he made me oblivious with his hands, he turned me on the tip of his finger … but I left; he said it to too many people.

He said 'I love you', but not to me. I left. I was not loved any more. Now he'd found another pair of eyes, another bosom; he was saying 'I love you' to them.

I was walking up and down the room. I just became aware of it. I was pacing, over and over.

I thought of Colin in bed with his curly-headed girlfriend. I didn't know her name. I wished I knew her damn name. I thought of our bed. How we'd bought it together one Saturday morning and taken it home, wobbling on top of the car. We'd carried it up the stairs and Colin had said, 'No, we must put it up immediately.' He always wanted things done like that, quickly: wanted them finished, so's he could stand back and look at them. He'd work and work on a programme, researching, filming editing, day and night, so he could look at it, the finished product.

I thought of the bedsheets. How I'd tie-dyed them one day in the launderette. Pushed them in knotted and tied, praying the attendant wouldn't see me dropping in the packets of dye and then leaning over the machine, covering the Perspex top with a magazine till I was faint with the heat, hoping she wouldn't come up and peer in like she sometimes did to make sure the washing was okay. She'd have seen bright purple soapsuds.

I thought of them lying in those sheets. Perhaps the girl saying, 'Lovely sheets you have,' and he'd say he bought them in a shop, or something. Or maybe he'd say, 'Oh I had a girlfriend once, she did them, but she walked out on me.' The girl would feel very sorry for him then. Put her head on his shoulder. 'Once I had a girlfriend and now she's gone. Buddy won't you spare a dime?' — that song.

I felt I was screaming. I stood at the end of the bed. My hands nailed round the brass railings.

I thought of Colin making love to her: his china hands, his body like wire. Would she be writhing and moaning out little cries? I thought, I'll never let anyone make love to me like that again. I'll never moan like that again, like an animal; they get you like an animal and then they laugh at you.

I grabbed my bag, keys (I still had one to his flat), money, cigarettes. I went down the stairs. Creeping. Please dear Jesus don't let Mr Maloney hear me. What would he think if he came out? I opened the big door; a swathe of cold air came in: the smell of the river. I'd forgotten my coat. If I go up, I thought, I'll surely disturb

Mr Maloney and his friend. I could see their startled faces looking round the kitchen door at a figure dressed in black satin with a rose in her hair leaping down the stairs at three in the morning.

The air was sharp. A wet, sharp blackness.

The taxi man's face hung in yellow folds from his receding hairline. 'Merciful Jesus,' he said, 'is it an apparition or what?' I smiled at him and he opened the door and the smell of the car came out—a cigarette smell.

I gave him the address. A stab of pain. Such a familiar address. Now his, and hers.

I shivered in the back seat. The taxi man threw back a plaid rug. It smelt of dogs and children; picnics at Dollymount probably and the kids sick from sunburn on the way home. I offered him a cigarette. He took it. He didn't ask questions. Didn't talk, just whistled 'The Ballad of James Connolly' through his teeth.

My mind was blank and yet full. Both. I couldn't think, in the sense that thoughts weren't going round my head one by one, orderly and shaped. I just felt this fullness that came out to the edges of my skull.

The town was so quiet. The trees—even the trees were still. The roads were quiet carpets to carry you through, the houses blank-faced—all those people in their beds, lying flat up on their little platforms, floor on top of floor of them, and all dressed up in their nightclothes, their day clothes silent in cupboards and on chairs. The houses gave nothing away. The houses said, 'Go by quickly; there is nothing for you here.'

The town smell was replaced by the sea smell. We drove on. The iodine of the seaweed banked in heaps under the seawall. During the day the seagulls strutted up and down: haughty, ugly creatures on the ground. In the air white whistles of light and movement, streaking through the sky. The sea that thrashed about with joy during the day was moving surreptitiously now, its secret concourse with the moon's power taking up all its energy.

The taxi pulled up. The taxi man leaned back his arm to open the door. I took out a pound. He gave me five shillings change. I gave him back his rug and said, 'Thanks a lot,' and he drove off, his winking red lights frivolous in the darkness.

I walked down the path. I had the key. The lights were all off. I let myself in, quietly, quietly …

The living room was the same; had I expected it different? A record was out of its cover. I put it back thinking, No point in having a good stereo if your records are scratched and clogged with dust. Businesslike thoughts like that. There was a plate on the table by the sofa, streaks of egg and bacon rinds: Colin's breakfast? He used to say breakfast was his favourite meal. An innocent meal.

I sat down on the sofa and lit a cigarette. The moon came slanting in. A girl's clothes lay on the floor; the moonlight lit them coldly. I went over. Tights and pants still together—she must have been in a hurry—a pretty dress, of course I remembered the dress; I'd seen it earlier that night in the restaurant. (Hours ago it seemed, hours.) It was black crepe with white broderie anglaise daisies sewn onto the shoulder straps. Very pretty on a thin girl. This one was thin all right. Colin wouldn't be seen dead with a fat girl, would he?

So. They were upstairs. They were in bed. I wondered which side of the bed she was on. Colin used to like to lie on the lamp side. Perhaps she was like that. Perhaps they had argued over it.

Mary said, 'Why always blame the girl?' I wasn't blaming the girl was I? How was the girl to know anyway? To know that Colin and I had been together for a year. That we had loved. Stupid things. Held each other's hands under the table at my father's house. Made love once in a cupboard at somebody's party; we couldn't wait. Bought things together, the bed for instance. She couldn't be expected to know all these things. Unless he told her. Did he tell her? Maybe she didn't care; why should she?

Anyway, if Colin wanted another girlfriend, then that was his business. I'd walked out, hadn't I?

Couldn't he have waited a bit?—for what?—till I got someone else? I didn't want anyone else. Mary said, 'Don't be daft, you will.'

But no, there is a person and for some reason you want that person to love you. You're a woman and he makes you more of one. That's love and you're told it over and over and all your life you've been waiting for it, watching for it. The more you're with him the more different you become. The more his, I suppose. But if he doesn't want you? If he only wants a bit of you? If he only wants you as he wants you and not as you think you might become—what then? If he says, 'Don't do this, or that; do this,' and says it over and over again until you can't remember when you last said, 'Right, this is what I'm going to do' and did it, then what?

I stood up. I walked up the stairs, quietly, quietly.

The bedroom door was open. The cupboards were open. Drawers open. Colin's clothes fallen round the room.

The bed. The bodies. His sprawled legs apart, on his back, his hair thick on the pillow. The smell. Woman's smell, man's smell. The smell of sex. Her body. Turned away from him, curled on her side, her face white in the moonlight.

I stood in the doorway. Time passed.

I turned and crept into the bathroom. Closed the door. Started—my face in the mirror, a mad painted face with staring eyes. I took the plastic bucket that I'd bought to soak our pants in. Filled it with water, slowly, quietly, shhing the water in.

I walked back to the bedroom. Opened the door. Looked. I thought. Every detail in this bedroom will stay in my mind for ever and always. Then I lifted the bucket waist high and flung the water over the two of them, over the bed, a soft transparent curtain of silk water curving through the air—

'Jeeesus Christ.' Colin jumped up.

'Oh, oh what's happening,' said the girl.

My heart jolted, turned over. I thought, Run, run, you stupid fool. My hand went up and flipped on the light. They were struggling, the girl's eyes squinting against the light, pulling the sheet around her, water dripping from her hair. Colin was leaning, straining up, on his elbows, kicking the bedclothes back: 'What the *hell* is going on?' he was shouting.

I said (my voice?), 'I just came back to tell you you're a bastard.' He was getting up to come over. I said, 'Don't come near me or I'll tear your eyes out.' I was faltering. What would I say? What could I say? They both looked white and scared, the girl particularly. I thought, Well what's the point? Suddenly I felt flat, winded, completely exhausted.

I turned out the light and started to run. Down the stairs out of the door and down the road. My footsteps were jolting in my head, *thrunk, thrunk*, the pavement hitting my face, running away. I thought, If he follows he'll kill me, and I ran and ran and my heart felt like a huge bellows pumping and straining. I started slowing down, turning my head, one hand holding up my dress. … turning … but no one was following. No one.

You're on your own now. Completely. The houses, blank, pass by quickly; nobody wants you here …

Or here …

Or here …

I sat in a shop doorway. The stone felt very cold. I'd no cigarettes. No key. I'd left my bag in the living room. Well, I thought, Well I'm very calm now, it's all over; I'm ready now, tomorrow I'll go and see Mary … I'll ask Mary about it … I'll start again. That's the thing—it's hard and complicated but you've got to start again, every time, never say dying.

Look at their damn faces lying there … the water curving and curling and their shouts … I began to laugh, my shoulders giggling with me, then to laugh out loud, the houses bending now, solicitous.

I thought: For God's sake, their damn faces streaming with water … and laughing and laughing … and I must stop this laughing soon and get going. But each time I thought of it …

My dear Colin, my dear love, and you, dear lady … well that can be your baptism.

And mine too … and mine.

∾ ∾

AFTERWORD

Writing is a peculiar business.

There I was, aged twenty-four, newly married and sitting in a whitewashed room in Africa, swags of bougainvillea tapping against the mosquito screens, writing about nuns, boys, boarding school and Ireland.

It was 1973, and I told no one, not even my brand new husband, what I was up to. I'd done enough time in McDaids, The Bailey, Davy Byrne's, seen enough novels-in-the-making talked into oblivion over hot whiskies, to be wise to that one. Oh yeah.

In 'silence, exile and cunning' I tapped away on my little aquamarine Olivetti and, manuscript completed, tied it up in a brown paper and string parcel in the post office in Dar Es Salaam, and sent it off to (impossibly faraway) London. A few weeks later a contract arrived from Michael Joseph. My tale of nuns and Ireland, boys and broken hearts, was going to be published.

Wow.

In Africa I was learning feminism backwards, frequently with rage attached. My brand new husband's recounting of sexual adventures, did not mean sauce for the goose being equally okay for the gander. Definitively not.

Outwardly I did all the things the 'Sisters' would have approved of – I had my own job, I didn't do his laundry, I talked the equality talk. Inwardly I was confused, angry, hurt. How *could* Prince Charming turn out to be such a bastard?

Unintentionally, I was living the reality of my heroine in *Fathers Come First*.

Looking back now, forty-two years later (*forty-two!*), it seems unbelievable that we convent-educated 'Nice Girls' were sent out into the world in such a state of naivety.

And, while Feminism had arrived in Ireland in the 1970s, it seemed few people actually *believed* in it. Feminism was a bit like bidets – all fine and good for a few 'poshies' in Dublin, but nothing to do with us ordinary people.

In real life it felt as if *all* of the rules favoured men. If a girl let a man (in truth usually a spotty boy) 'have his wicked way' on the first date i.e. touch her breasts, she was a whore. If a girl didn't let a guy touch her she was a 'frigid Brigid'. If a girl rang a guy after a date, she was 'fast'. If the guy didn't ring the girl back after a date, she was suicidal.

All the power in the world seemed vested in men, with the only access route to that power via men.

The men had the jobs, the money, the cars, the bank accounts.

We had sensationally short mini skirts (Is that a *pelmet* you're wearing? my darling Dad asked one sunny morning), and lots of feminist attitude, but in terms of worldly wisdom we were largely clueless.

What fun it would be to go back and tell my heroine Lizzie in *Fathers* that all will be well.

Oh Yes indeedy.